Except For A Staff

RANDY R. SPENCER

Except For A Staff

RANDY R. SPENCER

STARBURST PUBLISHERS

P.O. Box 4123, Lancaster, Pennsylvania 17604

To schedule Author appearances write:
Author Appearances, Starburst Promotions, P.O. Box 4123,
Lancaster, PA 17604 or call (717)-293-0939.

Credits:

Unless otherwise noted, all Scripture quotations are from the
New Scofield Bible, King James Version.

We, The Publisher and Author, declare that to the best of our knowledge
all material (quoted or not) contained herein is accurate; and we shall
not be held liable for the same.

EXCEPT FOR A STAFF

First Printing, November 1991

ISBN: 0-914984-34-9
Library of Congress Catalog Number 91-65976

Printed in the United States of America

Dedication

With much love,
I dedicate my first book to my wife,
Lynn,
who has faithfully and lovingly
encouraged me in the ministry.

Acknowledgments

I am exceedingly grateful to the members of Zion Baptist Church for their spiritual encouragement which inspired me to write this book, and without whose financial and prayerful support this vision would not have become a reality.

I am especially grateful to Jim and Nancy McLaughlin, who together faithfully persevered and shared in the task of grooming and editing the original manuscript throughout the various stages of writing. Special thanks to Shirley Smith and Brenda Over for the illustrations used throughout the book, and to Nancy Lewis for her poem.

I especially wish to thank Patrick McLaughlin, who I believe God directed into my ministry to administrate this great project. Without the unselfish contribution of his time, expertise, professional skills, and extensive editorial work, this book would not be possible.

To The Reader

In its theological sense, the word TYPE signifies truth connected with Christianity, such as an institution, historical event or person, ordained by God. Many types are identified in the New Testament, however, there are other types not specifically mentioned.

Contents

I Need A Staff (Poem)   VIII

Preface   IX

Introduction   13

1   The Power Of The Staff   21

2   Except A Staff, Only   39

3   A Staff Not Stuff   55

4   God's Men On Staff—Part I   65

5   God's Men On Staff—Part II   89

6   The Chosen Vessel   111

7   When The Staff Doesn't Work   139

8   She's Got A Good Little Horn   149

9   God's Broken Staff   155

I NEED A STAFF

Israel went out with a *staff* in their hand,
The sea rolled back and they crossed dry land.
With the *staff* in hand nothing ever seemed to go wrong,
It brought water from the rock, fire from the sky,
And miracles so mighty, no one dare deny,
It was the *Staff* of the Spirit that made God's people strong.

As Jesus left earth He gave a strange command,
"Go and win the lost with just a *staff* in your hand.
Leave everything behind, just take the *staff* along."
The disciples knew that they would not be alone.
The help that they needed would come from the Father's throne.
It was the *Staff* of the Spirit that made God's people strong.

It's the *Staff* of the Spirit that we need today,
For power in the battle and help when we pray.
It's a comfort for the weary as we sing the victory song.
It will help us to walk, and help us take a stand,
Guide us safely home to the Promised land.
It's the *Staff* of the Spirit that made God's people strong.

I need a *staff* when I preach; I need a *staff* when I pray.
I need a *staff* when I sing my song; it will drive my troubles away.
I need a *staff* when I walk; I need a *staff* to find my way.
It's the *Staff* of the Spirit that I need for my journey today.

Randy R. Spencer

Preface

Except For A Staff is a book dealing with a Biblical topic that will prove informative and unusually interesting to the Christian reader. I have reason to believe that similar material on this subject has never been printed, or if ever available, is no longer in print. To my knowledge, no one has written of the obviously striking parallel between the various functions of the Old Testatment shepherd's *staff* and the ever-present ministry of the Holy Spirit.

A careful study of the *staff*, an object mentioned repeatedly throughout the Bible, reveals it as a very significant spiritual symbol or type, somehow overlooked by the Christian world. The ancient *staff* was not merely an implement used by the shepherds but also was employed by rulers, teachers, travelers, the physically impaired, and warriors. In each instance, a more in-depth examination reveals that the specific use of this common stave, or rod, was intended by God to be a foreshadowing of the Holy Spirit. Numerous accounts in Scripture reveal this beautiful typology of the Spirit's ever-present ministry and manifest His true character. This intense study of the Old Testament *staff* sheds new light and a deeper understanding on the role of the Holy Spirit in the life of the Christian. Once the believer becomes aware of this obvious truth, it raises the question of why this insight has seemingly been overlooked.

There are multitudes of books written on the subject of the types of Christ revealed in the Old Testament, but one is hard pressed to find well-balanced truth on the subject of the symbols of the Holy Spirit, the Third Person of the

Trinity. It is my belief that if every believer became acquainted with this concept, the symbol of the shepherd's *staff* would become a familiar emblem: as familiar as the dove, the rainbow, the fish, and the cross. Just as the cross symbolizes the crucified Christ, the shepherd's *staff* should be a worldwide symbol of the empowering Holy Spirit, whose ministry provides comfort, rest, authority, support, defense, and much more. With proper exposure, the phrase "The *Staff* of the Spirit" should become a familiar expression known by Christians everywhere.

Ordained through the Independent Baptist Church, I have been in the ministry for over twenty years and have been involved in rapid church growth with an expanding radio ministry throughout the tri-state area in which I reside. I strongly believe that the heartfelt cry of the church is to receive a message that accurately exemplifies the true nature and ministry of the Holy Spirit. God's people today are hungering to know, based on sound Biblical truth, how the Spirit of God affects their lives.

The information contained in this book presents inspirational material for pastors and teachers and may be used as a series of messages that present to the believer a greater awareness of the anointing of the Holy Spirit. This book is written in an easy-to-read, anecdotal, personal testimony style, that applies truth through personal illustrations and stories.

Throughout my years of ministry, I have learned that the Scriptural messages I have delivered on the subject of the *staff* have been the most widely received and had the greatest impact on the lives of the Christians to whom they have been delivered. The insights addressed in this book have been shared with many men of God throughout the country, and every response has been the same: an overwhelming interest in learning more about these truths. Because many have urged and encouraged me to share this insight by way of the printed page, I have written *Except For A Staff.*

Introduction

In virtually every book of the Bible there are found various scriptures containing a wealth of beautiful types and portrayals of Christ. It has been said: "Christ is in the Old Testament concealed, in the New Testament revealed." Although many people are familiar with the passages relating to Christ, it is not with equal familiarity that they recognize the Person and ministry of the Holy Spirit.

At first glance, the types and portrayals of the Holy Spirit, as portrayed in the Old Testament books of the Law and Prophets, may seem rare and ambiguous. However, upon closer inspection, the ministry and Person of the Holy Spirit can be found throughout the Old Testament.

Through this book I would like you to gain an understanding of the manifestation of the Holy Spirit as shown in the pages of the Old Testament. It is my desire that God will reveal to you, as He has to me, the type of the Holy Spirit that is found in an obscure and seemingly insignificant, primitive implement, known as a *staff*. Within the shadow of this *staff* is revealed the third Person of the Trinity, true to His very nature and character, working unnoticed, offering guidance, powerful assistance, and gentle, loving reproof to all who would recognize His presence.

There are many misunderstandings and misconceptions today concerning the ministry of the Holy Spirit. I am convinced that these errors could quickly be resolved if we would recognize the lovely portrayals of the Holy Spirit in the Old Testament *staff*. Many scholars overlook the significance of what is described in the Scriptures as a simple shepherd's *staff*, when in essence it sets forth a wonderful typology of the Holy Spirit and truly foreshadows His future ministry. A study of the physical uses of the Old Testament *staff* reveals the nature of the spiritual ministry and workings of the Holy Spirit in the New Testament.

In my research for this book, I have discovered over 250 references to the *staff* in the Bible. In most instances, the *staff* was a physical sign with much greater spiritual implication. Today, the physical *staff* found in the hands of the Old Testament prophets has been replaced by the spiritual *staff*, the Holy Spirit, as found in the New Testament. That which God's men once held securely in their hands was placed much more securely in their hearts.

I believe one of the most devastating and costly mistakes made by the evangelical church of today is its nearly conscious denial of the deity of the Holy Spirit. During the earlier days of church history, there was a position taken by some churches that led to the devastating effects known as *liberalism*. Many churches began to deny the deity of Christ, resulting in their spiritual decay and death. Today, many of these mainline denominational churches openly deny the fundamentals of the faith: the virgin birth; the inerrancy, infallibility, and verbal inspiration of the scriptures; the literal death, burial and resurrection of Jesus Christ; the new birth experience; and the second coming of Christ. These churches have degenerated into mere social clubs and religious organizations, empty and devoid of any spiritual blessings from God. As a result of their denial of the true ministry of Jesus Christ, "Ichabod," meaning "the glory of the Lord hath departed," could very well be written over their doors. In the same way that liberalism, formalistic orthodoxy, and modernism have removed the blood of Jesus from the salvation experience, many evangelicals have removed the anointing and convicting power of the Holy Spirit. While one has done a great injustice to Christ and His work, the other has done an equal disservice to the work of the Holy Spirit. This reveals that what is needed today is a fresh, new anointing of the Holy Spirit, an unction from the Holy One (1 John 2:27; 2 Corinthians 1:21-22).

This is why I have a deep concern for the evangelical churches of today. There are those within our own camp who have made the tragic error of rejecting the truth of the deity of the Holy Spirit. They refuse to honor the Holy Spirit, the third Person of the Trinity, and fail to recognize His Lordship within the Church. While those of us who call ourselves *Fundamentalists* take pride in the fact that we hold to the fundamental truths of the Scripture, including the person and work of the Lord Jesus Christ, we often fail to see the fundamental nature of the doctrine of the Holy Spirit. Do we honestly realize *who* it is that we are ignoring when we refuse to allow the Holy Spirit His rightful place of ministry in the church and in our lives? Yes, the Holy Spirit, the Third Person of the Divine Godhead who is ever present in the heart and life of every blood-bought believer, is directly working in the affairs of men.

Allow me to make one clear distinction before I proceed any further on this subject. Since the theme of this book focuses on the indwelling dynamics of the Holy Spirit, it is imperative that I make clear my doctrinal position and then continue to build upon that foundation. According to the Word of God, every believer is born of the Spirit (John 3:3-6; 1 John 5:1), indwelt by the Spirit (1 Cor. 6:19, Gal. 4:6; 1 John 2:27), and sealed by the Spirit at salvation (Eph.1:13; 4:30). Then why is it necessary for the believer to prayerfully seek the Holy Spirit when He has already taken up His residence at salvation? Being indwelt by the Holy Spirit, He possesses us. Every believer is indwelt by the Holy Spirit at salvation, but not necessarily empowered for service at that time. One *cannot* be saved apart from the personal work and indwelling of the Holy Spirit:

> *But ye are not in the flesh but in the Spirit, if so be that the Spirit of God dwell in you. Now if any man have not the Spirit of Christ, he is none of his* (Romans 8:9).

It is not my intention to become involved in a long theological discourse on the doctrine of the Holy Spirit. May it suffice to say that much of Paul the Apostle's writings were intended for New Testament Christians as instruction on how to be filled, controlled, and empowered by the indwelling Spirit. It is clearly obvious that many Christians are not living in the power of the Spirit. When I make reference to the importance of the believer receiving the *staff* of the Spirit, I am referring to the special anointing for service, not the indwelling for salvation.

There is much discussion and controversy today about "the baptism of the Holy Spirit." That being what it may, there is, however, one work of the Holy Spirit that is irrefutable and imperative, and that is for the necessities of power, purity, and performance in service to our Lord. You may choose your own terminology, but I prefer to call it "My Staff." Furthermore, ponder if you will the words of one of the spiritual giants of the faith, A.W. Tozer, "Now I know that some say I have confused people about the blessings of the Holy Spirit and in answer I want to point out that if the Lord's people were only half as eager to be filled with the Spirit as they are to prove that you can't be filled with the Spirit, the church would be crowded out."[1]

I am convinced that many churches today are no longer operating in the power of the Spirit of God. That is why they are formal, cold, ritualistic, liturgical, and dead. No visible signs of spiritual life appear in their midst. Shouts of praise? Unheard of! "Joyful sounds unto the Lord" are so faint they wouldn't even wake up the proverbial "church mouse." Enthusiasm for winning the lost to Christ has disappeared, having been replaced by banquets, parties, social gatherings, etc.—all in the name of "Christian fellowship." The sound of a hearty "Amen!" today would prove embarrassing to many, including pastors who no longer preach with emotions or power. There is an absence of tears at the altar, accompanied by a lack of heartfelt joy. All of these things, and many more, are indicators of the lack of supernatural power. The average Christian has very little understanding of true worship.

Many spiritually discerning, Bible-believing Christians would never admit that they have done an injustice to the person and work of the Holy Spirit. But the absence of anointing on their ministries testifies to the fact that there is something wrong. This denial has not come by way of an open doctrinal statement, but subtly, through the use of creeds and oaths of loyalty to a particular church or organization. Such creeds render the influence of the Holy Spirit as "unnecessary" and "impractical," precluding the possibility for a victorious daily walk. The emphasis upon the influence of the Holy Spirit is so vague it is almost nonexistent among church members today. I believe that if God chose today to entirely remove the presence of the

Comforter (the Holy Spirit), that 90% of all churches would continue to function as though nothing happened. Most Christians would continue on with "business as usual."

What has caused Bible-believing Christians to become so insensitive, fearful, and even antagonistic toward the ministry of the Holy Spirit? If there is such a thing as a simple answer to this question, it's probably found in the fear of being identified with the "wrong group." There is no doubt in my mind that the modern-day "Holy Ghost Explosion" has done much damage through a misrepresentation of the true ministry of the Spirit of God. This tidal wave of error, accompanied by the misinterpretation of scriptures, fleshly performances, unbiblical practices, indigent behavior, and pandemonium has caused many spiritually discerning Christians to be wary of anything identified with the name of the Holy Ghost. Many church leaders have taken such a strong stand against "emotionalism" that believers fear any kind of display of feeling or emotion. This fear of "emotionalism" has reaped the whirlwind of spiritual deadness: no tears, nor joyous laughter, nor heartfelt shouts or amens; no clapping of the hands, nor friendly smiles, nor outward expressions of feeling; and no spirit!

Sadly, many who have taken issue against this "exhibitionism" have become extremists in the opposite direction. Fearful of being labeled pew-jumping, aisle-running, holy-rollers, they have grieved, quenched, and robbed the Holy Spirit of His true ministry.

I think the sense of "wonder," spoken of in the New Testament and enjoyed by the early Christian church, remains one of God's priorities for every Christian living in this Church Age. God has not changed concerning his people. He is the same yesterday, today, and forever. There was a constant feeling of joyous expectation among believers throughout the New Testament. Daily, God's people experienced the power and blessings of God, extending far beyond their expectations. Yet the church today seems to have lost that wonder and excitement.

Perhaps we need to take the time and effort to approach the Lord before entering into the worship service, to seek an outpouring of His spontaneous blessings via His Spirit, that our cups may be filled. How many of us are willing to take the time to do this? Let's be honest, the first thing most of us do when we arrive for the worship service is read the bulletin to see what blessings man has already planned for us. Is it any wonder His people leave the service with empty cups and empty hearts?

If the Spirit of God desired something special for your church, would He first have to meet with the church board, prearrange the service, and have the program typed in the bulletin?

Does your spirit "bear witness with His Spirit?" Do you have the assurance that what you possess in your spiritual life is all that God promised and intended for you when He sent His Spirit to dwell in you?

I want to challenge God's people to return to a balanced truth, with a renewed commitment toward God's demonstration of His ability to bring about the movement, freedom, and operation of His Spirit. I realize, that even in the writing of this book, many will not even extend to me the courtesy and fairness of reading these pages with an open mind; but instead, will quickly draw conclusions and put a label upon me. My greatest desire and purpose in this writing is to challenge you, the reader, to search your heart and sincerely ask yourself: Have I allowed the *Holy Spirit* His rightful place in my life and ministry? I trust that our

consideration of the shepherd's *staff* as a type of the Holy
Spirit will yield fresh insights as it relates to the person,
nature and work of the Spirit of God.

[1] Taken from the book, *When He Is Come* by A. W. Tozer, Copyright ©1968
Christian Publications, Camp Hill, Pennsylvania. Used by permission.

chapter 1

The Power Of The Staff

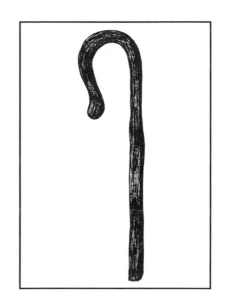

Power! The very mention of the word brings an air of fascination, wonder, and suspense. Probably, it is the single most sought after property or distinction on earth, even more so than wealth, fame, or wisdom; for by the mere possession of power all other desires are easily obtained. From the very dawn of recorded history, humans have fallen prey to its deception and alluring enticements. It was this pursuit of power that led our original parents in the garden of Eden to disobey God and eat of the forbidden fruit with expectations that in doing so, *they would become as God* (Genesis 3:5). Later in time, fallen man made another attempt to "make a name" for himself by building a city and a tower *whose top may reach unto heaven* (Genesis 11:4). Even before the fall of man was the fall of Lucifer, who in his own quest for power, tried to overthrow God and determined, *I will be like the Most High* (Isaiah 14:14). What is it in the heart of humanity that causes such infatuation with dominance, power, or control? What is the fire raging in the heart of man in this unquenchable thirst for power? What causes even a small boy to stand in wide-eyed wonder as he gazes at the body builder whose physique ripples with muscle? What is so fascinating about guns and the world renowned .44 magnum, "the most powerful handgun in the world?" Why the box office sellouts for movies like *Rambo, Rocky, Commando* or any of a dozen movies on the martial arts? Is there some kind of innate desire to be successful, powerful, or simply a "winner?" The ever increasing quest for power careens out of control on the world's scene. The struggle between the world's superpowers continues to rage over the "arms race." Since the beginning of time, political leaders have sought world domination. Could it be that even Alexander the Great's lust for power wasn't quenched when he cried in desperation, "There are no more worlds to conquer!" Even the Christian world is vulnerable to this deceptive struggle to attain success or become successful. Still fresh in our minds are the memories of the religious kingdoms which recently crumbled and became an open reproach to the Christian church. We look askance at some church leaders today who are seemingly in a power struggle to accumulate great wealth or build their own personal empire.

But what is power? Who is the most powerful? Is power in the hands of the one holding the most weapons? Is strength in nuclear warheads, ballistic missiles, or the megaton bomb? What is more powerful than a cobalt bomb, which in theory can destroy the entire globe if one is placed at each of the poles and detonated, or more accurate than a laser beam which with microscopic precision can etch the entire *Lord's Prayer* on the head of a pin, or more complex than the human brain which activates millions of brain cells simultaneously? Or what is faster than the spy plane, the SR-71 "Blackbird," recently taken out of active service, whose top speed is classified information?

Yet the reality remains that power is fleeting and vain! There is always someone or something better and more powerful. The champion never retains his title. His is only one-time power, and it will always be overcome or surpassed.

I believe every individual has his own concept of power. I remember being fascinated as a young teenage boy by the power of automobiles. I grew up in a day when drag racing was popular, and every kid dreamed of owning a "hot set of wheels." The ultimate feeling of power was in sitting behind the wheel of a drag racer that was "souped to the gills." The drag strips and speedways were roaring with excitement in the '60s. I especially remember "Nu-Bee" in New Bethlehem, Pennsylvania; Keystone Drag Strip near Pittsburgh, Pennsylvania; and just a few short miles from my home was Hummingbird Speedway, Ohio. It was never enough to just go watch the "power wagons" speeding down the tracks. No, every young boy had to own one. Regardless of whatever piece of junk one could possibly acquire or afford, he had to soup up the engine to get maximum performance. So expressions like: horsepower, headers, solid lifters, traction bars, side pipes, bored-out to the gills with chrome rings, Mallory ignition, and a pair of four-barrel carbs, all spelled "POWER." The sound of roaring engines and squealing tires were music to my ears.

I was fortunate enough to have a younger brother, Al, who also shared this obsession for powerful cars. Al owned a '63 Chevelle that was a drag racer's dream. Al practiced long and hard to get all the drag racing techniques just right. He knew how to burn-out, speed-shift, and rev that 396 motor to its "max." I can still recall the conversation one Saturday afternoon between Al and our dad. Dad knew that Al spent a lot of time in the garage working on his car, and he knew Al was "hot rodding." However, to a man that grew up in horse and buggy days, and the days of the Model T, hot rodding was breaking 50 mph. The argument, or should I say conversation, was based upon the subject of speed and power. Dad had just purchased a new car, a pink Rambler with a 250 horsepower motor and a 3 speed automatic transmission. To him, that was a hot car! Now certainly Dad was not into drag races or speedways, but he was convinced that his Rambler could beat anything on the highway; and of course, Al argued and accused Dad of not knowing what real power was all about. Thus went the argument, until Al finally talked Dad into going with him—just one time through the quarter-mile in his Chevelle. Dad finally agreed. I couldn't believe it! There we were, headed to the quarter-mile strip with Al behind the wheel, Dad in the front seat, and me in the back. I knew what was coming. I'd been there many times, and it's frightening. I'm sure Dad was thinking, "What can you do in a quarter-mile, maybe break 55 mph." Well, after a few burn-outs to soften up the rubber, Al pulled to the line, revved that 396 to its maximum rpms, and dumped the clutch. The roar of the engine screaming was deafening, the tires were howling, and the forward thrust shoved us back so hard that it felt like you were going through the upholstery. It sounded like a loud crack of lightning as Al speed-shifted through each gear and fought to keep the old Chevelle from fish-tailing out of control. I glanced at

Dad in the front seat as Al hit third gear, and noticed the color drained from his face as his head snapped against the headrest.

The great thing about our Dad was that he always did everything with us boys. Whatever we would do, he was always "one of boys," but this was one time he had overstepped himself. He would never admit he was scared or made a mistake. He always kept a cool head to get himself out of any situation. As Al hit fourth gear and the speedometer was reaching the 90's, Dad peeled himself from the bucket seat, reached over, and turned off the key. And, as cool as he could, he said, "Now, boy, a good motor like this should not be abused. When you treat this car right, I'll give you your keys back." Yet another one of those "unforgettable moments" at the Spencers', but a valuable lesson was learned: power is not made to be abused.

Today, 25 years later, I still myself fascinated with power, but a much different "Power." The power that I long to see manifest in my life is the power of the Holy Spirit. This power was promised to every believer in Acts 1:8, *But ye shall receive power, after the Holy Spirit is come upon you . . .* It is to this power that I dedicated my book. The hour has come when we, the Church, must exercise this supernatural power. If we are to stand in this last day, it will be through the power of the Spirit. The arm of the flesh will not sustain God's people in the critical hour that we face. For too long the world has viewed the Church as weak, anemic, and fragmentary. The day is come when the world must see a supernatural, God-empowered Church that even the very gates of Hell cannot prevail against. God assures us that we cannot perform in the flesh what He wants to do in His Spirit.

Except the Lord build the house, they labor in vain that build it; except the Lord keep the city, the watchman waketh but in vain (Psalm 127:1).

I must agree with my Dad. "Power like this must not be abused." The Holy Spirit is in essence the motor of the Church. And if we are going anywhere, it will be when we give proper attention and respect to this great motor. Sometimes I see a Church which carelessly and recklessly abuses and flaunts God's power for its own glory or fleshly gratification. Other times, I see a Church which ignores the power of God, almost afraid of what will happen if it exercises that power. We sometimes have all the spiritual machinery, but without the oil of the Holy Spirit, this great machinery will surely fail! We must understand our responsibilities and commitments to the power of the Spirit, and be able to handle it as mature Christians.

The Holy Spirit is an everlasting power, a force that causes all other power to fall helpless in His presence. If we wish to view the operation of the most powerful element on earth and in the universe, we will not see it in the nuclear warhead, or in the Star Wars initiative, or in Saturn rockets, or microchips, or in hydroelectric current. In the midst of all our searching for modern and scientific sources of power, Let us go to the Old Testament and pull from its types and images a rather obscure, primitive "ole stick," and propose this to be the most powerful tool known to mankind and an apt emblem of the power of the Holy Spirit. It is called the "Shepherd's Staff." I challenge you to consider it a manifestation of the ultimate source of power which supersedes all that man's intelligence and technological prowess can muster.

What is a *staff?* In today's era of rapid travel, the *staff* seems somewhat obsolete. In the age of jets, ocean liners, space shuttles, trains, buses, automobiles, elevators and escalators, there is very little need of a "walking stick." In a matter of hours, a person can travel anywhere in the world, and hardly take a step. By traveling faster than sound, if you're not careful, you might find yourself arriving before you left! In the place of bunions and blisters, we get "jet lag."

One would also be hard-pressed in America to find a shepherd with a *staff*, standing in a field keeping watch over his flock. Is it any wonder that most of us have never seen a genuine shepherd's *staff*? And to be quite frank, probably no one really cares to see one. Asked to describe what a *staff* is, we would have to draw from what we were told as children growing up in Sunday School, or from what we've seen in Bible pictures, or in a Bible drama on television. Although the *staff* seems as old as Moses, and as lost as sheep in a wilderness, it still has great significance for modern man. Because the *staff* is so unfamiliar and foreign to most of us—allow me to dig it up, dust it off, and introduce you to one of the most valuable, priceless tools Christians could ever hold onto. I believe it would be wise for every Christian to more fully understand the significance of the *staff* and the power it represents.

Your initial reaction may be that a *staff* seems a very insignificant and unimportant object to devote a whole book to. Most would think of it as a simple ancient tool used solely for shepherding. However, I have discovered its miraculous power and deep spiritual significance to be very prominently displayed throughout the Old Testament. My research has shown that it is mentioned over 250 times in the Holy Scriptures. Let us now turn our attention to some of those references which reveal the true meaning of the *staff.*

The Hebrew word *matteh* is translated as "rod, *staff*, shaft, or branch." The basic meaning of *matteh* is "*staff*." The Greek work *rhabdos*, which is the Septuagint rendering of *matteh*, can also be translated "*staff* or staves," which simply means a sharp-pointed stick. This same Greek word is used for "rod," and signifies a piece of tree limb used as a support or as a weapon. As I searched deeper into the scriptures, I found even more varied uses of this ancient and very familiar piece of equipment. Jacob used the *staff* to change the color of Laban's goats and sheep (Genesis 30:36-41). Also, the *staff* was used as a symbol of authority or as a scepter (Hebrews 1:8). Men and animals were disciplined or smote with them (Exodus 21:20, Numbers 22:27, and 1 Samuel 17:40). We can infer that grain was sometimes beaten out with the *staff* (Judges 6:11 and Ruth 2:17). The *staff* was used by the people for support or defense (Exodus 21:19 and Zechariah 8:4), and also used by travelers as walking sticks (Genesis 32:10, Exodus 12:11, and Matthew 10:10). As I read of each of these physical functions of the *staff*, I can see beautiful implications, symbols, emblems, and types of the Holy Spirit unfolding into spiritual applications. It is quite interesting how these two words, *matteh* and *rhabdos*, are used in the Old Testament scriptures. After I began my word study, what I found most striking was how a parallel could be drawn between the use of the *staff* in ancient times and the present-day ministry of the Holy Spirit—revealing, in fact, that the *staff* is a typology of the Spirit! Have you ever considered that the *staff* referred to in the Bible has a much greater significance? Could this simple, crude, shepherd's tool mentioned on numerous occasions throughout the Bible actually hold some special symbolic meaning? Yes it can. I believe that in every reference to the *staff* throughout the Old and New

Testaments there are types of the Holy Spirit which carry implications for us as believers, and have generally gone overlooked in past investigations.

One of the first accounts of the use of the *staff* is in Genesis, Chapter 38, where Judah, a shepherd, gave his *staff* to his daughter-in-law, Tamar. This *staff* was left with Tamar as a surety that he would keep his promise and return with a kid from the flock. Verse 18 reads:

> *And he said, What pledge shall I give thee? And she said, Thy signet, and thy bracelets, and thy* **staff** *that is in thine hand.*

Likewise, we Christians have a promise from the Lord that He will return, just as he promised (Joel 2:28-29; Zechariah 12:10; John 14:16, 26).

The *staff* was also a symbol of authority. God gave Assyria His *"staff"* as He commissioned Assyria to go in God's power and carry His sword into battle. Isaiah 10:5-6 says,

> *O Assyrian, the rod of mine anger, the* **staff** *in whose hand is mine indignation. I will send him against an hypocritical nation, and against the people of my wrath will I command him, to take the spoil, and to take the prey, and to tread them down like the mire of the streets.*

Also in the Psalms and in the books of the Prophets, it is repeatedly mentioned that when God sets up His Messianic kingdom during the Millennium that He will rule with a strong *"staff"* or "rod." *The Lord shall send the rod of thy strength out of Zion* (Psalms 110:2). Our spiritual scepter today, likewise, is in the Holy Spirit. Jesus gave that authority to us before He left and commissioned the believers to do His work. (See Acts 1:8; 20:28).

The *staff* was also an ancient means of defense:

> *Thou didst strike through with his own staves* (staff) *the head of his villages; they came out like a whirlwind to scatter me . . .* (Habakkuk 3:14).

We know, as Christians, that our warfare is not a physical
one, but rather a spiritual battle (Ephesians 6:12), and the
weapon we use to defeat the enemy is the Spirit and His
"sword" (Ephesians 6:17).

The Old Testament *staff* was a means of demonstrating
power, or was used in performing miracles. Aaron's rod
budded to authenticate his priesthood. Moses' rod, turned
serpent, swallowed Jannes' and Jambres' rods. The Egyptian
magicians used *"staffs"* as symbols of the powers of the
magical realm by which they counterfeited Moses' miracle
(Exodus 7:12). We know that genuine miracles only come
from the Spirit of God as the scriptures testify in Acts 8:13.
The people watched in amazement the ministry of Phillip:

> ... *beholding the miracles and signs which were
> done* ... *And when Simon saw that through laying on of
> the apostles' hands the Holy Spirit was given, he offered
> them money, saying, Give me also this power* ... (verses
> 13b, 18-19a).

The Holy Spirit was the early Church's source of power,
and He is our source of power today to help us pray, serve,
witness, and live a victorious life (Acts 1:8; 2:1-4; Luke
24:49).

Furthermore, we find the staff being used as a prodding
stick to guide and move herds in certain directions. Men
and women, as well as animals, were goaded by the *staff*
(Exodus 21:20; Numbers 22:27; 1 Samuel 17:43). The sharp
stabs or pricks of the *staff* were used on many occasions
to bring correction and guidance to the flock to keep them
from straying. Thus the Holy Spirit will prick our hearts
today, and use the sharp stabs of conviction to direct us
to Christ (Acts 2:37; Revelation 22:17).

> *And when he is come, he will reprove the world of sin,
> and of righteousness, and of judgment* (John 16:8).

Thus far, we have seen the *staff* being used by rulers, warriors, magicians, and farmers. Let us note further the use of the *staff* as teacher. 2 Samuel 7:14, reads:

> *I will be his father, and he shall be my son. If he commit iniquity, I will chasten him with the rod (staff) of men . . .*

Proverbs mentions, on numerous occasions, the use of the "rod" in child training or discipline: *He that spareth his rod hateth his son . . .* (Proverbs 13:24); *The rod and reproof give wisdom . . .* (Proverbs 29:15). The rod, or *staff*, was used to give direction or training to the son, or student. The basic use of the rod was not necessarily for beating, but rather for instruction and direction.

> *But the anointing which ye received of him abideth in you, and ye need not that any man teach you; but as the same annointing teacheth you of all things, and is truth, and is no lie, and even as it hath taught you, ye shall abide in him* (1 John 2:27).

See also John 14:26; 1 John 2:20; Luke 12:12; and John 16:13.

The *staff* is also found in the hand of every person overcome by the vicissitudes of life. Those that had been beset by the world used it to give themselves support and rest. In Exodus 21:18-19, we read of the judgments of the law for personal injuries caused to others. These verses specifically deal with the punishment given to one who smote another and caused injury. Verse 19 reads:

> *If he rise again, and walk abroad upon his staff, then shall he that smote him be clear: only he shall pay for the loss of his time . . . .*

According to the law, if a man smote (hit) another and he died, that man should also be put to death; but if the one smitten were crippled and could move about upon a *staff*, then restitution was made for his lost wages. The point I wish to make is simply this—those injured in life used the *staff* as an aid for recovery and as that which would aid them in their continued endeavors. In the New Testament, when the Church was hampered through persecution, as recorded in Acts, the Holy Spirit ministered as a comforter and helper enabling the church to triumph. Acts 9:31 states,

> *Then had the churches rest throughout all Judaea and Galilee and Samaria, and were edified; and walking in the fear of the Lord, and in the comfort of the Holy Spirit, were multiplied.*

Therefore, the Holy Spirit may be viewed as a spiritual support for any who may be maimed in the spiritual warfare of life.

The *staff* was also found in the hand of every traveler to assist as a simple walking stick. In Genesis 32:10 Jacob, as he traveled, said *for with my staff I passed over this Jordan* . . . Likewise, the Holy Spirit becomes the "walking stick" for every believer, or pilgrim. We are pilgrims in this life and, therefore, called to *walk in the Spirit* (Galatians 5:16, 25; Romans 8:1).

Finally, the *staff* was owned and carried by everyone— from the youngest to the oldest. Zechariah 8:4 says,

> *Thus saith the Lord of hosts: There shall yet old men and old women dwell in the streets of Jerusalem, and every man with his **staff** in his hand for very age.*

The *staff* was certainly a very common item in ancient Jerusalem. It was just as common to see people holding a *staff* then as it is to see people wearing shoes now.

Today, the Christian is personally indwelt by the Holy Spirit, and every believer has the promise of His presence. I can claim the Holy Spirit as mine, personally! He was not generally given to the whole world, nor collectively to the whole church, but each blood-bought believer is a temple for Him in His fullness. I don't have just a part, or portion, of the Holy Spirit, but rather enjoy and claim Him wholly as mine (Acts 2:1-4,17; Romans 8:9; 1 Corinthians 3:16; John 14:17).

I believe that it is now obvious to each reader that the *staff* was more than a mere shepherd's tool. We have seen the *staff* in the hand of rulers, warriors, magicians, farmers, travelers, the imperiled, and the common man. It was, without a doubt, a very familiar implement to all, and had many varied uses. However, I do not intend to neglect the most important use of the *staff* as a shepherd's tool, and have reserved the latter portion of this chapter to discuss it. I hope through this discussion that, above all, it will become clear that the *staff* is an emblem of the Holy Spirit, foreshadowing His work in the life of each believer.

The *staff* is much more than a long stick with a crook or hook on the top that the shepherds of old used to guide their sheep. When we look at shepherd lore, we find every shepherd took special pride in the selection of a staff that was just right for him—exactly suited to his own size, strength, and personal use. This long, slender, primitive piece of equipment was so necessary to the shepherd who could carry only the barest essentials. The staff became a fixed part of every shepherd, a permanent attachment with him. It was a precious comfort to the shepherd as he wearily leaned on it for support. Furthermore, the *staff* of the shepherd was an indispensable aid in climbing hills, beating down brush, driving off beasts of prey, and directing straying sheep. However, no other single word could better describe the function of the staff than that of comfort. For we read in Psalms 23:4, *Thy rod and thy staff they COMFORT me.* That word, comfort, is the very word that Jesus used to describe the Holy Spirit:

> *But the Comfort(er), who is the Holy Spirit, whom the*
> *Father will send in my name, he shall teach you all*
> *things . . .* (John 14:26).

Jesus places into the hand of the believer a comforting *staff* that offers sweetness, consolation, and a gentle, loving relationship. Through the Holy Spirit, His "*Staff,*" Jesus shepherds us every day of our lives.

As is with most people, I knew very little about shepherding, so I couldn't speak through experience or firsthand knowledge until I began this study, but, in the process, I have read and heard that the *staff* was used for three significant roles. Please allow me to quote from Philip Keller's book, *A Shepherd Looks at Psalm 23.* Philip Keller is equipped with a shepherd's experience and personal insight, and he clearly describes the three areas of sheep management in which the *staff* plays a most significant role:

> "The first of these lies in drawing sheep together into an intimate relationship. The shepherd will use his *staff* to gently lift a newborn lamb and bring it to its mother if they become separated. He does this because he does not wish to have the ewe reject her offspring if it bears the odor of his hands upon it. I have watched skilled shepherds moving swiftly with their *staffs* amongst thousands of ewes that were lambing simultaneously. With deft but gentle strokes the newborn lambs are lifted and placed side by side with their dams. It is a touching sight that can hold one spellbound for hours. But in precisely the same way, the *staff* is used by the shepherd to reach out and catch individual sheep, young or old, and draw them close for intimate examination. The *staff* is very useful in this way

for the shy and timid sheep that normally tend to keep at a distance from the shepherd.

"The *staff* is also used for guiding sheep. Again and again, I have seen a shepherd use his *staff* to guide his sheep gently into a new path or through some gate or along dangerous, difficult routes. He does not use it actually to beat the beast. Rather, the tip of the long slender stick is laid gently against the animal's side and pressure applied guides the sheep in the way the owner wants it to go. Thus the sheep is assured of its proper path . . .

"Another common occurrence was to find sheep stuck fast in labyrinths of wild roses or brambles where they had pushed in to find a few stray mouthfuls of green grass. Soon the thorns were so hooked in their wool they could not possibly pull free, tug as they might. Only the use of a *staff* could free them from their entanglement."[1]

This is a beautiful portrait, depicting the importance of the shepherd's *staff!* But the spiritual implications are even more fascinating and beautiful, as we see the *staff* of the Holy Spirit drawing each of us close to the bosom of the Father.

We read in Psalm 95:7,

For he is our God, and we are the people of his pasture, and the sheep of his hand.

. . . we are his people, and the sheep of his pasture
(Psalm 100:3).

All we like sheep have gone astray; we have turned every one to his own way . . . (Isaiah 53:6).

In like manner as the physical shepherd's *staff* drew, guided, and rescued the sheep—so also is the ministry of the Holy Spirit. As the *staff* drew the sheep together, guided them into new paths, and rescued them from precarious situations, so also the Spirit of God draws men to God:

> *No man can come to me, except the Father, who hath sent me, draw him* (John 6:44);

He guides them through the paths of life:

> *Nevertheless, when he, the Spirit of truth, is come, he will guide you into all truth* (John 16:13);

and rescues or preserves them:

> *Those that thou gavest me I have kept, and none of them is lost* (John 17:12).

Oh, what a magnificent analogy is drawn between the shepherd's *staff* and the Spirit of God, our Comforter. I'll secure Him tightly and rest in this my sweet comfort and consolation! For He is my *staff!*

In ancient days the *staff* was, without a doubt, a very familiar implement to all, and had many varied uses. It was certainly the most practical and powerful tool one could possess. Today, the *staff* continues to represent the ministry of the Holy Spirit, and I would readily submit to you that He, the Holy Spirit, is likewise the most practical and powerful tool a Christian can possess! If we would fully grasp this *Staff* of the Spirit, it would soon be broadcast that we now secure the most powerful force on the earth! A power that cannot be attained through payment, performance, or presumption, but rather through prevailing prayer. The Power of the Spirit!

As I mentioned earlier, I found it very enlightening as I did a brief word study in the Greek language in both the Septuagint (Greek translation of the Old Testament) and New Testament to find the word *staff* (*rhabdos*) also translated *rod*. Although the Greek word *rhabdos* could be simply translated *stick*, it was also translated into any one of the following words: *staff*, stick, rod, staves, wand, or switch, depending on the *specific* use. Therefore, I believe we have an accurate analogy in the Bible between the specialized translations of the Greek and Hebrew words for *staff* and the various ministries to the believer by the Holy Spirit. With this brief synopsis of the *Staff*, let's look now to the scripture that initially sparked my interest in writing this book.

---

[1] Taken from the book, *A Shepherd Looks At Psalm 23* by W. Phillip Keller, Copyright ©1970 by W. Phillip Keller, Zondervan Publishing House, Grand Rapids, Michigan, Used by permission.

chapter 2

Except A Staff, Only

*And commanded them that they should take
nothing for their journey, except a **staff** only . . .*

Mark 6:8

Let us momentarily leave the Old Testatment and go
to the New Testament to Mark 6:7-13 where the *staff* is
once again mentioned:

> *And he (Jesus) called unto the twelve, and began to
> send them forth by two and two, and gave them authority
> over unclean spirits; And commanded them that they should
> take nothing for their journey, except a **staff** only; no bag,
> no bread, no money in their purse: But be shod with sandals;
> and not put on two coats. And he said unto them, In
> whatever place ye enter an house, there abide till ye depart*

from that place. And whosoever shall not receive you, nor hear you, when ye depart from there, shake off the dust under your feet for a testimony against them. Verily I say unto to you, It shall be more tolerable for Sodom and Gomorrah in the day of judgment, than for that city. And they went out, and preached that men should repent. And they cast out many demons, and anointed with oil many that were sick, and healed them.

Take nothing for the journey except a *staff?* A very unusual request indeed!

This passage, like every passage of Scripture, is given for a specific reason. This is verified in 2 Timothy 3:16:

All scripture is given by inspiration of God, and is profitable for doctrine, for reproof, for correction, for instruction in righteousness.

Wherein lies the reason for this particular portion of scripture?

In order to better understand the specific instruction given here to the Twelve, we will cautiously proceed through these verses to discover what valuable insights the Spirit of God wishes to reveal. Let's begin with the focus on the CONTEXT of this event.

Keep in mind that Jesus knew His earthly ministry would soon end as the imminency of the cross drew near. He would no longer be with His disciples in bodily form. They themselves had not yet fully comprehended the fact that Jesus, in order to fulfill Old Testament scriptures, would soon be put to death and that their lives would be greatly changed. These twelve had left all to follow Jesus; their jobs, their homes, their friends, and their personal ambitions in life, and became totally dependent upon Him. The one who had lovingly provided for their every need—financial, emotional, spiritual, physical, and material would soon depart from them by way of the cross. When they needed food, he multiplied the loaves and fishes; when Peter needed money for the the temple tax, Jesus supplied that need by means of a coin found in the mouth of a fish which Peter caught; and when the disciples needed protection, he rescued them from each and every perilous situation. In every circumstance, their needs were securely provided by the Lord Himself.

Previously, the disciples had spent much time alone with the Master. They sat at His feet, listened to His teaching, and saw His miracles. Now, Jesus, knowing that His departure was drawing near, was concerned that the disciples must learn dependence upon the Holy Spirit, who would descend from Heaven following His ascension. This is borne out in John 14:16-19 where Jesus said,

> And I will pray the Father, and he shall give you another Comforter (provider), that he may abide with you forever; Even the Spirit of truth, whom the world cannot receive, because it seeth him not, neither knoweth him, but ye know him: for he dwelleth with you, and shall be in you . . . Yet a little while, and the world seeth me no more . . . .

Jesus was preparing the hearts of the disciples for the descent of the Holy Spirit, who would take His place of earthly ministry. Major transitions were developing which would affect the lives of all believers, present and future; from the spiritual nurturing of the heavenly Father in the Old Testament, to the physical embrace of Jesus during His earthly ministry, to finally, the sustaining ministry provided by the Third Person of the Trinity, the Holy Spirit, which would continue throughout the duration of the church age. The disciples must learn quickly that Jesus would no longer continue walking with them in His physical form. They must learn to depend upon another power, another provision—the Holy Spirit. In order to teach this very important lesson to His disciples, Jesus brought a very precarious set of circumstances into their lives.

Now in light of the CONTEXT, let us look at the COMMISSION given. Jesus called His disciples together and issued forth the commission found in Mark 6:7:

> And he called unto him the twelve, and began to send them forth by two and two, and gave them authority over unclean spirits.

They were about to embark upon their first solo flight! The disciples had been taught by Jesus, and now they must teach others His Gospel. Consequently, they were sent forth on a missionary journey.

Their commission was no different than ours today. We are commanded of God to go into all the world, to every creature, to preach and teach the Gospel message. Yes, the burden of the Great Commission still weighs heavily upon the shoulders of every believer.

> And Jesus came and spoke unto them, saying, All authority is given unto me in heaven and in earth. Go ye, therefore, and teach all nations, baptizing them in the name of the Father, and of the Son, and of the Holy Spirit, Teaching them to observe all things whatsoever I have commanded you; and, lo, I am with you always, even unto the end of the age. Amen (Matthew 28:18-20).

Do you see in the latter part of the verse the specific promise of Jesus to go with us? How can he accompany us if He's no longer present on the earth? He uses His agent, the Holy Spirit.

Continuing in Mark 16:15-18, further instructions of this commission are given to Christ's followers.

> And he said unto them, Go ye into all the world, and preach the gospel to every creature. He that believeth and is baptized shall be saved; but he that believeth not shall be damned. And these signs shall follow those who believe:

> *In my name shall they cast out demons; they shall speak*
> *with new tongues; they shall take up serpents; and if they*
> *drink any deadly thing, it shall not hurt them; they shall*
> *lay hands on the sick, and they shall recover.*

The disciples were given specific orders to go among the heathen, as lambs among wolves, to perform the impossible—enter into every village, town, city, and continent, and eventually unto the uttermost parts of the earth with the Gospel of Jesus Christ. What a task for twelve men!

The commission given to the disciples to carry on the identical work Jesus had done during His earthly ministry causes me to reflect upon the words found in John 14:12:

> *Verily, verily, I say unto you, He that believeth on me,*
> *the works that I do shall he do also; and greater works*
> *than these shall he do, because I go unto my Father.*

Fellow-believers, we are likewise commissioned to continue His work. And what is His work? Isaiah 61:1,2 clearly defines it:

> *The Spirit of the Lord God is upon me, because the*
> *Lord hath anointed me to **preach good tidings** unto the*
> *meek; he hath sent me to bind up the brokenhearted, to*
> *proclaim liberty to the captives, and the opening of the*
> *prison to those who are bound; To proclaim the acceptable*
> *year of the Lord, and the day of vengeance of our God;*
> *to comfort all that mourn; To appoint unto those who*
> *mourn in Zion, to give unto them beauty for ashes, the*
> *oil of joy for mourning, the garment of praise for the spirit*
> *of heaviness . . . .*

Have we lost sight of our calling and commission today? Is the Great Commission of preaching and teaching, binding up the brokenhearted, proclaiming liberty, opening prison doors to those who are bound, etc., being carried out as it was given?

As I observe many ministries today, I see conversely people who are placed under bondage, legalism proclaimed instead of freedom, guilt in place of comfort, and injury inflicted where wounds should be bound up. There's no oil of joy, no garment of praise, and there is the absence of the preaching of good tidings.

Many of our colleges and seminaries today are commissioning young men into ministry solely on the basis of theological suppositions or doctrinal hypotheses. Some Bible scholars are more knowledgeable about *exegesis* than they are about Jesus. They can recite from memory the Apostle's Creed, but are ignorant on the subject of winning the lost. They can convincingly argue the five points of Calvinism or oppose Armenianism, but not know how to deliver the captive from his bondage of sin. They have extended vocabularies, and use phraseology such as "Anthropomorphic representation of the immutability of God," but it's beneath their dignity to say, "Hallelujah" or "Amen!" Many are scholars in the fields of Pneumatology, Eschatology, Soteriology, Hamartialogy, and Ecclesiology, but lack the ability to comfort those who mourn. They can teach about the "hypostatic nature and the impeccability of Christ," but have hidden flaws in their own lives.

Obviously, they have all the humanly and institutionally required credentials, but lack the necessary spiritual essentials. **A parchment without passion is useless. The call of candidates to the ministry should not be determined by the acquisiton of a Master's Degree, but by the degree to which they have met the Master.** Many pulpits today are filled with Doctors of Divinity who are, sadly enough, unable to prescribe the spiritual medicine that heals the broken heart.

I recently spoke with a frustrated young minister who

related to me the events which led to his entering the ministry. He had graduated from a well-known theological seminary, having completed six years of study and earning the all-important Master's Degree. He was confident he was adequately prepared for his first church. He had all the right answers, but no one asked him the right questions. He quickly discovered that his parishioners were not even remotely impressed with all his intellectual knowledge. He had prepared his dissertation on the "Dispensational Divisions of Human History," but no one requested his rhetorical hermeneutics. The little country church he was pastoring simply wanted someone to love them, feed them, comfort them, heal their spiritual wounds, and tell them about Jesus. It could be stated succinctly by saying more is taught by our lives than by our lips. Precept must become practice, illustration must lead to experience, and indoctrination to inspiration.

Please do not misunderstand. I am not against, but favor education. I have earned a Bachelor's Degree, and am presently completing work toward a Master's Degree. Helpful as these may be, they are not the top priorities for the success of my ministry. In the discussion which follows, I will describe what I, personally, believe to be the most necessary ingredient for carrying out the Great Commission.

Having considered the CONTEXT and the COMMIS-SION, let us now consider the COMMAND. Mark 6:8 says,

And (Jesus) commanded them that they should take nothing for their journey, except a staff only; no bag, no bread, no money in their purse: But be shod with sandals; and not put on two coats.

What a seemingly preposterous command. Could this be right? Such meager provisions for such a great undertaking?

Logic implies that the greater the task, the greater the need for provisions. TAKE NOTHING! How absurd! Inevitably, the question arises as to how they could possibly survive on this long journey without adequate supplies. What possible provisions would be necessary for such an endeavor? Their master, who was mindful of their every spiritual, physical, and financial need, would certainly not forsake them now! Surely this Christ thought of everything they would need on this audacious journey. Imagine how you would feel if you were commanded to travel by faith alone, without benefit of any previous arrangements— reservations, money, etc.

A closer inspection of the Scriptures reveals that the Twelve weren't really traveling empty-handed. Unaware of its significance, there was one very important item they took with them. Verse 8 identifies it: *Except a staff only.*

We've examined the CONTEXT, the COMMISSION, and the COMMAND. Now let us proceed in examing the COMMODITY.

There was one commodity that Jesus deemed necessary for their journey—a *staff*. One might facetiously question, "Lord, this ole walking stick? Will it keep me warm on cold nights? Will it provide something to eat when I'm hungry? Will it provide rest for my head when I am weary and worn?" Now, this is not the first occasion on which God had given this simple *staff* with admonition, "This is all that is neccessary for the journey." We read in earlier accounts where God's chosen men of might and power had eventually learned the lesson of reliance upon this *staff.*

Was our Lord negligent concerning the needs of the disciples? On the contrary. The disciples were not aware that the *staff* they were told to take along on their journey was a palpable symbol of the Holy Spirit, which would prove sufficient for all their needs. The emphasis upon the importance of the physical *staff* was the instrument Jesus used to teach the disciples the importance of leaning upon the spiritual *staff*—the Holy Spirit.

The purpose for Christ's unusual command was simple— since the *staff* was such a prominent and practical implement in the lives of the disciples, it portrayed the spiritual power which was to come. Jesus was simply setting forth a fundamental truth for the ministry of the church. The *staff*, representing the Holy Spirit, was absolutely imperative for all Christian workers. God used the physical *staff*, so familiar to the disciples, as a foreshadowing of the power which was to come. Jesus was not only teaching the early disciples dependence upon the Holy Spirit for power and provision, but was also setting a pattern for His servants throughout the ages. Now we understand how Jesus could make such a promise as:

> *and lo, I am with you always, even unto the end of the age* (Matthew 28:20).

Yes, what God's people held in their hands would soon be placed in their hearts through the indwelling Spirit, to abide throughout ages to come.

Sending forth his apostles, Jesus had the power to provide for them with every material provision conceivable, but chose rather to teach an unforgettable principle of truth. Without the *Staff of the Spirit*, all other material means would prove insufficient. With the *Staff of the Spirit*, God alone proves to be our all-sufficient need. The physical *staff* in the hand of each disciple was a picture of the believer in the forthcoming ages, launching forth in service with the power and anointing of the Holy Spirit.

What we need for effective ministries today is the endowment of God's power, the Spirit of the *staff*. The missing commodity today in many ministries is Power! Luke 24:49 states:

> *And, behold, I send the promise of my Father upon you; but tarry ye in the city of Jerusalem, until ye be endued with power from on high.*

The disciples were instructed to go to Jerusalem and wait for the arrival of the Spirit. In the present-day Church Age, we need not delay nor tarry, for the promise of the Father has already come.

At Pentecost, the Spirit of God descended to take up His residence in the hearts of believers, and become their source of power, provision, protection, and presence. Acts 1:8 states:

> *But ye shall receive power, after the Holy Spirit is come upon you; and ye shall be witnesses unto me both in Jerusalem, and in all Judea, and in Samaria, and unto the uttermost parts of the earth.*

How shall we ever fulfill the command of the Great Commission? Only by the power given unto us through the Holy Spirit—*Except For A Staff.*

The need in the church today is for a greater emphasis upon the essentials and a minimizing of incidentals, stressing the spiritual and placing the material in its useful, but proper place. The material is convenient but not essential; practical, but not primary; and favorable but not fundamental.

Once the disciples recognized the Holy Spirit as their Sustainer and Provider, Jesus permitted an enhancement of their ministries through use of material provisions.

> *And he (Jesus) said unto them, When I sent you without purse, and bag, and shoes, lacked ye anything? And they said NOTHING! Then said he unto them, But now, he that hath a purse, let him take it, and likewise his bag; and he that hath no sword, let him sell his garment, and buy one* (Luke 22: 35-36).

Once the disciples had learned the intended lesson of dependence upon the *staff*, they were then given the privilege of useful supplementals.

We need educated men in the pulpits, necessary tools to aid in the operation of the ministry, and funds to meet the expenses. However, without the oil of the Holy Spirit, the machinery within the church produces little or nothing. We need God's holy unction to function! Jesus was emphasizing the importance of venturing forth only under the authority and dynamic power of the Holy Spirit.

Today, both the church and Christians suffer and are often ineffective, because we have lost sight of what God considers most imperative for the ministry. Our priorities are out of order, and we major on the minor, rather than majoring on the true necessities. What tools does God declare to be essential for the tasks we are sent forth to accomplish?

From this unusual passage in Mark's gospel we have considered the CONTEXT, the COMMISSION, the COMMAND, the COMMODITY, and now let us conclude this chapter with the CONSEQUENCE. What were the results of the disciples' ministry, when they traveled with so little? Were they successful? Did they lack anything? Were they in danger? What did they accomplish? (Recall, in Luke 22:36 where Jesus asked, *Did you lack anything?* And they said, *Nothing.*)

A study of Mark 6:10-13 reveals the disciples' preaching led to men repenting, the powers of demonic bondage being broken, and the sick being healed. In contrast to other scriptural accounts, it is recorded that great miracles occurred as blind eyes were opened, the lame were made to walk, the deaf to hear again, and sinners were converted. Without doubt, their first evangelistic tour was an overwhelming success!

One example of the many successes within their mission can be found in Acts 3:1-11, where the first apostolic miracle occurred. Peter and John had gone up together into the temple to pray. A man, who had been lame from birth, was lying at the gate of the temple seeking alms. When asked for money, Peter replied:

> *Silver and gold have I none, but, such as I have, give I thee. In the name of Jesus Christ of Nazareth, rise up and walk.*

The lame man immediately received strength and healing, and entered with Peter and John into the temple *walking, and leaping, and praising God.*

Oh, the impact of Peter's statement when he said, "We have no money, but we have the Power of God." Dear reader, the church's treasury today is full of silver and gold, but it is bankrupt in power. When the sick, lame, blind, and halt cry today for healing and deliverance, we offer them money . . . "such as I have, give I thee." What a poor substitute!

Praise God, that seemingly insignificant stick (the *staff*) continues to work. And its working results in unbelievable success and fruitfulness.

To reiterate, they took nothing, and everything happened; we can take everything, and nothing happens. Has the church ever been so fully equipped? We either own, or have access to, more tools for the work of evangelizing the world than ever before in human history. Think of the advantages we have today through modern technology. The outreach of the gospel message is not limited by man's own faculties. The modern FAX machine makes it possible to extend our arm by way of nerves of wire, resulting in a printed message being transmitted instantly anywhere on earth. Likewise, via telephone, radio waves, and satellites, our voices are transmitted anywhere in the world, including outer space.

Today, by use of modern technology, it's simple to communicate with humans on the moon. Yet sometimes we experience difficulty in conversing with our next door neighbor. Today man's eyesight seems to have no limitations. In a recent article . . . "Tokyo (AFP)":

"The overall Experimental Laboratories of Tokyo's University engineering department has developed the world's most powerful microscope," the department announced. "It's resolving power is 500,000 times—enlarging a needle's hole to the size of a baseball stadium." [1]

There is an unusual article that appears in the book entitled *Encyclopedia of 7700 Illustrations*, which reads as follows:

"Imagine a man stepping over parked cars, uprooting a tree, carrying a telephone pole up a cliff, or racing through an impassable swamp. Scientists at General Electric's advanced technology laboratory in Schenectady, New York, are making this possible.

"They've designed the Pedipulator, a seventeen-foot-high robot skelton. A man will stand inside the Pedipulator's 'skull' and manipulate the machine through his own arm and leg movements. The Pedipulator will amplify the normal power of the man's limbs many times over, enabling the man to perform Superman feats.

"The man may lift his leg as though he were stepping over a parked car. If a tree stands in his way, the man need only grasp it with his super-arms, pull gently, and the tree will come out by the roots.

"The developers are enthusiastic. One says, 'It's extremely difficult to teach a robot to do things. But this joins man and machine. Then you have man's brain and nervous system joined to the machine's great strength.' " [2]

James C. Hefley

Despite man's efforts in the technological development of any, and all, kinds of gadgets and devices which make life easier and more convenient, one simple truth still remains: God does not use machinery or systems, but rather, men. Jesus invested His life in the lives of twelve men who would turn their world upside down for the Kingdom of God. How can we do anything less?

I believe these are critical days in which God uses faithful servants to perform His tasks. These servants may develop useful systems, but the converse is never God's intention. God never calls, or uses, systems to meet human needs. He always calls people, and equips them with the Power to perform the task. Dwight L. Moody once said, "God is always looking for men who are little enough to be big for God." If Christians would just submit themselves to the authority of His Spirit and act as His representatives of this authority, I am firmly convinced it would instill within each one of us more self-confidence and produce immeasurable results.

As an illustration, I recall an incident that happened several years ago. I was having trouble with my automobile. On several occasions, I had taken it to the garage to be fixed. Yet, each time there seemed to be no noticeable change. Finally, on my fourth visit to the same garage, with the same problem, I said, "You have tuned it, adjusted it, calibrated it, and analyzed it; now, this time will you just simply fix it?" Of course, I was only jesting, but the

truth remains—like anyone else, all I really wanted was
for it to work. This simple illustration exemplifies what
is needed in our churches today. Less analyzing and
organizing, and more implementing of the One who is
needed to make it work—the Holy Spirit.

To some, it may seem trite to say that we need to depend
upon the power of the Holy Spirit, but it is the missing
element in many of our churches today. There is heaped
upon our hands the only solution suitable to meet the needs
of people. God help us if we don't use it or apply it effectively.

*Are ye so foolish? Having begun in the Spirit, are ye
now made perfect by the flesh* (Galatians 3:3)?

In these last days, anointed men and women are needed
as God's human instruments for reaching a needy world.
If you or I can be that instrument, in whom is found the
Staff of the Spirit, then we should be willing to readily make
ourselves available for His service. God has offered it. We
can accept it or reject it, and live with the consequences
of our decision.

Called into the ministry at the youthful age of 15, I felt
a strong tugging at my heart, and was eager to learn what
God required of me for full-time service. I learned in the
earlier years of my ministry that I was nothing and He
was everything. I stood empty-handed before God and said,
"Lord, I am available. I have little to offer, but what I
have I give to You . . . please use me." The often quoted
verse, "Little is much, when God is in it," aptly describes
the ensuing years of my ministry.

I have learned that for everything God expects of me,
and for every problem or enemy that rises up against me,
He has lovingly and properly prepared me to meet the
challenge—with *staff* in hand.

[1] *Encyclopedia of 7700 Illustrations* by Paul Lee Tan, Th.D., Copyright ©1979 by Paul Lee Tan, Th.D.; Assurance Publishers, P.O. Box 753, Rockville, Maryland 20851, Article 6449, p 1433.

[2] Ibid, Article 6452, p. 1434.

chapter 3

A
Staff
Not
Stuff

As the apostles began their ministry with only a *staff*, so also God endeavors to bring every true servant of Christ to that same level of dependence upon Him. Such was the case for me when I took those first spiritual steps into the ministry. I think almost all of us can relate to humble beginnings—especially those beginning years of your marriage when life is filled with financial hardships. It is a truism that "struggle builds character," and God must have had that in mind when He allowed my wife and me to get married my last year of college.

When I met Lynn, my wife-to-be, I was a junior at Appalachian Bible College in Bradley, West Virginia. I had decided that I was not going to leave college without finding a good "helpmate." I obviously had more than books on my mind when I enrolled at Appalachian Bible College!

Even though I did have one more year of college to complete, I was ready to get married after finding the right one. I've always been very aggressive. I felt once I had her on the hook I better land her before she got away.

So that summer, Lynn and I talked about marriage. But all the talk would not remove the many obstacles to our becoming man and wife. First of all, the school had a policy requiring any students who married to drop out of school for one year. Second, I needed additional financial support for my last year of school; and third, if we were to get married, we needed jobs and an apartment near the school.

We had only two months in which to solve these problems before the opening of school. Lynn and I, therefore, prayed and asked the Lord to meet these needs if He wanted us to be married.

Within two weeks, the answer to our first dilemma came in the mailbox. I received a shocking newsletter from the college which solved the problem of married students having to withdraw from school. The governing board of the college had met over the summer and revised some of the school policies. The officials had voted that a student may return the following semester after he married, if the student was twenty-one years old. And guess what? In just three weeks I would celebrate my twenty-first birthday. Hallelujah! God worked mightily in our lives!

What a miracle that was. I couldn't have been more shocked and amazed. Could God actually be in this whole crazy idea of getting married before I graduated? It was exciting; but how was God going to meet the next need? I had never experienced receiving a large sum of money before, and unless God met the financial need, I certainly could never undertake my final year of college. Incidentally, no one but Lynn and I knew about our prayer and plans to get married before school started. It was totally up to the Lord at that point, and approximately two weeks later, the second answer came. God spoke to the heart of a very precious man to give me an envelope with 10 one-hundred dollar bills enclosed. That man remains anonymous to this day, but I still praise the Lord that he was willing to be obedient to God.

Back in the early 70's, a thousand dollars was a tremendous amount of money. And with additional help from my parents, I certainly had no problems with school bills.

By then I became convinced that God could and would provide for all my needs. Certainly he had his job cut out for Him as I ventured off to school with a little cash in my pocket and a whole lot of faith and confidence that God is sovereign.

The last need was met as Lynn and I traveled to Bradley, West Virginia, in search of an apartment and employment. By God's grace, we found a small two-room apartment in town. Lynn was hired at a local cafeteria for thirty-five dollars a week, and I was able to work at the Seven-Up Bottling Plant in the evenings for thirty dollars a week. With the apartment secured and the promise of employment, we headed back to Pennsylvania to get married before school started. On August 15, three days after my twenty-first birthday, wedding bells were ringing in the little brown church in Chestnut Grove, Pennsylvania.

A few days later we loaded the '63 Rambler with all our earthly belongings and headed for Bradley, West Virginia. Everything we owned in this world was in the back seat and trunk of that car. But, regardless of our meager possessions, we had something far greater than the wealth of this world; we had absolute peace that God was also in that car with us. He had directed us together and he had proven to us His will for our lives. With God's blessing on our marriage, we started a journey with His anointing— nothing else could be more wonderful.

Oh, what a consolation, knowing that one's life partner has been chosen by God, and to know that when conflicts and trouble enter into marriage, there is one truth we cannot escape or ignore: together we are in God's perfect will; apart, we are out of His will. That has been a solid rock in which we have anchored for twenty years of marriage. Would to God that all young couples could determine to place a fleece before the Lord and let God give them a clear sign of His perfect will.

It was certainly not easy that last year of college and first year of marriage. But God's faithfulness was continually evident. Many times I had to coast the Rambler down the hills to save on gasoline. There were weeks we lived on frozen pot pies, four for ninety-nine cents, and leftover pastries from where Lynn worked. There were times we had to search for a few coins in the car seats to have money to do the laundry. But one thing was certain, God's presence was ever-abiding. He never failed to meet an exact need in His precious timing.

I remember planning a long trip back home to Pennsylvania to visit my family, and figuring out to the exact dollar how much gasoline it would take to get there and back. I said in jest to Lynn, "Well, if we get caught in one too many stop lights, we will never make it back." Those were the good old days, when absolute faith in God was being exercised. More "seasoned" Christians would call it foolishness. I called it faith! It's all we had, and God never let us down!

Payday was coming soon, and Lynn and I had made plans to travel to Luthersburg, that weekend. We were so excited to get home again to see the whole family, and because there was no school on Monday, we would have a long weekend. I was paid twenty-five dollars from the Seven-Up Plant on Thursday, and Lynn had her two weeks earnings coming on Friday. I would pick her up at 5:00 p.m. and we would leave immediately. I had used up all my money—including my paycheck on Thursday, to pay the next month's rent and remaining bills. Lynn's wages of seventy-five dollars would be plenty to make the trip home, and we would still have enough to live on until the next payday. After my morning classes, I spent the rest of the day on Friday getting ready to leave, and anxiously awaited five o'clock so I might pick Lynn up at Angie's Cafeteria. We would go to the market at the mall, pick up a few snacks for the trip, and cash Lynn's check at the counter. Then we would stop and get the tank filled with gasoline and head out. Great plan! I was always good at mapping out the order of events.

Things seemed to go exactly as planned. I picked Lynn up and sat in the car while she went into the market to cash her check. Soon we'd be on our way! Lynn exited the market with the grocery bag in hand and got in the car. I started off for the gas station, when Lynn let out a scream: "My money is missing! It's gone! Where is it?" Of course, I went through a whole chaotic litany of exclamations, "Look in the other pocket! Look in the shopping bag! Maybe you put it in the glove compartment! You didn't drop it, did you? Lynn, think!"

We quickly raced back to the market only to come up empty-handed and extremely frustrated. Apparently, Lynn had laid the cash on the counter while she packed the grocery items, and someone after her took the money. The clerk said she saw the cash, but thought it belonged to the lady behind Lynn. Needless to say, our jubilant trip came to a sudden end. We returned home, and sat on the edge of the sofa—crying. Nothing could be done!

We called Mom and Dad and told them we would be unable to visit them. It's difficult to convey in words just how much disappointment and hurt one really feels in such times. However, once again God's peace came in like a flood. That night before we went to sleep, we prayed together, believing God must have a reason for allowing this to happen. How could we be bitter or angry? We were trusting in a God who knows all things. He even knows things before they happen. Could God have saved our lives from some tragedy that might have happened on the way home? We made a million guesses, but it was simply not our place to question God.

"I don't need to understand, I just need to hold His hand." That's exactly what we did that night. Though disappointed and upset, we simply held the hand of our Saviour. We found the strong arms of Jesus holding us and His sweet presence assuring us that everything would be fine. What might seem a small matter to someone else was a devastating and disappointing event in our lives at the time. We look back at it now and chuckle, to think of all that God has brought us through since those days. But the little lessons were God's way of preparing for the much greater trials ahead.

We were awakened the next morning by a knock on the door. Much to our amazement, there stood my family. They were also very disappointed that we could not make it home, so after receiving our call, they decided to leave immediately and traveled all night to make a surprise visit.

God was so good to us, and that weekend was so special. Not only had God reassured us of his love once again, but I had a fresh reminder of my family's love as well.

Incidentally, the next day Dad and I were getting ready to get in my car when Dad noticed a large pool of transmission fluid flowing from underneath the chassis. I later learned that the transmission had a serious leak and according to the mechanic, we would not have made it half of the way home. The car would have given out in no time. I could not imagine being stranded along the desolate highways in West Virginia at two or three in the morning. But God could! He loves us so much. God also provided for the repair of the transmission. I'm so glad I walk by faith and not by fate!

What I did not understand at the time was that God was equipping us to trust in Him for another journey— a much more vital one—the journey into the ministry. It would have its disappointing trials, and many times the road would be rough, but God was introducing me to His "walking stick," a *staff* which was so necessary for the journey. It would be that "walking stick" that would keep me from falling and failing on life's journey.

God was saying, "I don't want you loaded down with unnecessary incidentals." He wanted me to learn early in my ministry to stress the spiritual, and to put the material in its proper place and perspective. God puts power and effectiveness first and foremost. Money, gasoline, food, and clothing are secondary in His idea of equipment. Take what you need of them, and more will be provided as you go. Venture not forth in service without the faith, authority, and dynamics of the divine Holy Spirit. It is God we need above and beyond anything else imaginable. Substance alone is insufficient. Material wealth without the Maker constitutes a miserable dilemma. Spare time, extra fuel, and a fat bank account are only a burden to him who knows not the excellency of God's power and provision.

It is interesting and enlightening to learn what is indispensable and what is unnecessary for life's real service. All the *stuff* of the world cannot begin to replace the *staff* of God. Paul the apostle, learned that there was no substitute for the dynamics of the Spirit that cause the heart to burn and faith in God to grow. Paul learned in his many journeys, and in prisons, that the essentials in life are really few: the simplest of food and shelter, covering the body—and above all—God's presence. Paul says it well:

> *I have learned, in whatever state I am, in this to be content* (Philippians 4:11).

> *At my first defense no man stood with me, but all men forsook me; I pray God that it may not be laid to their charge. Notwithstanding, the Lord stood with me and strengthened me, that by me the preaching might be fully known* . . . (2 Timothy 4:16-17).

How would you like to admit that your faith in God is exercised when every other alternative has been exhausted? How many of us find it necessary, when we plan for a long trip, to first count out several hundred dollars in cash to take along in case of emergency? We line up our stack of credit cards to pay for everything from gasoline to dinner. We make sure all our major credit cards are safely tucked away, our membership to the AAA Auto Club is still in effect, and run the car to the nearest garage to have a mechanic go over everything to make sure it's mechanically sound.

Once the travel route maps we ordered have arrived, we check with the weather bureau for road conditions and make necessary motel reservations. Finally, we're ready to venture out. God help us—in our "don't leave home without it" society—we virtually leave Him totally out of our preparations. In a generation of Master Card, Visa, AAA, and First Nationals, we must not forget a living God who promised to:

> *supply all your need according to his riches in glory by Christ Jesus* (Philippians 4:19).

It's seemingly a lot easier to trust in Master Charge than to trust the Master-in-Charge.

God longs to provide for His children as they go in His glad service. He honors the adventurous and obedient spirit with a bed at night and breakfast at day break. With the Holy Spirit, a *staff* is plenty; without Him, we accomplish nothing of lasting value.

If we cannot trust God for the necessities of life, how in the world will we ever trust Him for power to serve? Please do not misunderstand my point. I certainly do not embrace a philosophy of indifference to our everyday material needs, nor am I implying that we should face every situation of life unprepared, and blindly or ignorantly expect God to do everything for us. But I do strongly suggest to you that our priorities today are in need of drastic revision.

Happy is the heart that has learned to look to God above for His power, presence, provision, and protection. I praise God for my formal education and the benefits of a college degree; however, a college or seminary degree can never replace prevailing prayer and the power of God's Spirit. I'll never cease to praise God for enrolling me in the school of the Holy Spirit where I got my "foremost degree." The one course of study I'll always remember is: the *staff* is better than the *stuff*.

chapter 4

God's
Men
On
Staff

Part I

As I pondered the text in Mark 6, and pictured those apostles walking away from Jesus with "only a *staff*," my eyes opened to a Bible truth that I had never seen before. Fascinated, I began to read throughout the Scriptures, and noticed that every great man of God held a rod, or *staff*, in his hand.

Before the Holy Spirit was given in Acts 2, all men of God carried a physical *staff*, rod, or stave as an outward sign to all nations and peoples that the Holy Spirit was dwelling upon them. Even though they knew not the person of the Holy Spirit, it was the Spirit that gave them the power to perform the great works that God called them to do.

The physical presence of a *staff* in hand was a spiritual sign of God's presence. It was God's way of saying, "Without me you can do nothing." However, because the Holy Spirit was sent to earth in Acts 2, we now have no need of a physical *staff* as a sign; for now the Spirit of God not only abides with us, but He dwells within us. The Spirit of God does not simply come upon men today as in the Old Testament, but at the time of conversion to Christ, He comes into us.

The heart of the Christian becomes the temple of God (1 Corinthians 3:16; Romans 8:11). Jesus spoke about this in John 14:16,17 when He said:

> *And I will pray the Father, and he shall give you another Comforter, that he may abide with you forever; Even the Spirit of truth, whom the world cannot receive, because it seeth him not, neither knoweth him: but ye know him; for he dwelleth with you, and shall be in you.*

At Jesus' ascension, He told the disciples to go to Jerusalem and tarry there until the Spirit would be given to them for their long journey of service. He said in Luke 24:49:

> *And, behold, I send the promise of my Father upon you: but tarry ye in the city of Jerusalem, until ye be endued with power from on high.*

In Acts 2, we find the disciples tarrying in Jerusalem, as Jesus had instructed them, waiting for the promise of the Holy Spirit—their "walking stick," their new *staff.*

Jesus removed the physical *staff* from their hands and gave to them a spiritual *staff* for their hearts. His urgent warning was still the same, "Don't go out without it." He says in Acts 1:8:

*But ye shall receive power, after the Holy Spirit is come
upon you; and ye shall be witnesses unto me both in
Jerusalem, and in all Judaea, and in Samaria, and unto
the uttermost part of the earth.*

The *staff* or Spirit would be absolutely essential for power
in service to the Master. It would be their strength to walk
upright, a comfort to their hearts, to defend them against
the enemy; their tool to perform miracles, the supplier of
their spiritual water and bread, and the very means by which
they could rescue and save the lost sheep. What was once
in their hand was now placed much more securely in their
hearts.

Let us now turn our attention to a few of these men
whom God employed and equipped with the *staff*. Whom
God employs, he also equips. Allow me to introduce to
you "God's Men on Staff!"

Jacob

With my staff I passed over this Jordan.
Genesis 32:10

When we come to the life of Jacob, that great man of
God whom God so mightily used, we see the *staff* of God
at work. Renamed Israel, for he would be the father of
a great nation, he served his time in the school of the Holy
Spirit, in the land of Haran where he served his future father-
in-law for twenty years. He needed this schooling because
he held to the very popular misconception that, if you are
to get ahead in this life, you must look out for number
one, i.e., yourself. The philosophy which believes that if
you want the good things of life, you have to lie, cheat,
and steal to obtain them. Jacob wanted the blessing of Isaac,
his father, so he planned a way to steal his brother Esau's
birthright. In the 27th chapter of the book of Genesis, the

story of his deceit is recorded in graphic detail. After Jacob succeeds with his scheme, he is found running for fear of his life, and meets his deserving reward in Padanaram by getting a good dose of his own bitter medicine. He found that deception, double dealings, duplicity, and guile were no way to prosper with God.

After twenty long years in God's school of hard knocks, Jacob was ready to graduate with honors awarded in the form of a *staff*. God had finally broken Jacob, and reduced him to a mere slave, serving a cunning and deceitful taskmaster. It was in that land that God stripped Jacob of every earthly possession and honor, and restored the *staff* into his hand. Now Jacob must return to his country and face his brother, Esau, whom he had wronged and cheated so many years before. We read in chapter 32: 9,10:

> *And Jacob said, O God of my father, Abraham, and God of my father, Isaac, the Lord who saidst unto me, Return unto thy country, and to thy kindred, and I will deal well with thee; I am not worthy of the least of all the mercies, and of all the truth, which thou has shown unto thy servant; for with my staff I passed over this Jordan; and now I am become two bands.*

What a difference in attitude as Jacob returns. When he left, he was proud, arrogant, greedy and deceitful; now a broken man returns to his brother to make restitution.

God reassures Jacob that with *staff* in hand he *will make (his) seed as the sand of the sea, which cannot be numbered* (Genesis 32:12). When will we learn that all the lying, scheming, deceptive, delusive, fraudulent acts will never afford us a high position or prosperity? But with a simple *staff* in hand, God will bless our lives with such abundance that we cannot contain it all.

Before we leave Jacob, there is something very interesting to which I direct your attention. Once Jacob realized the value of the *staff* of the Spirit, he gripped it tightly and securely for the rest of his life. For we read in the New Testament, Hebrews 11:21:

> *By faith Jacob, when he was dying, blessed both the sons of Joseph, and worshiped, leaning upon the top of his staff.*

Why in the limited pages of Holy Scripture would God direct the writer of Hebrews to mention such a trivial thing? But is it? When you realize what the *staff* meant to the Old Testament saints, and how it pictured the precious Spirit of God, this passage takes on new meaning.

After walking all those miles with God's Spirit as his aid, Jacob, now weary and weak, tired and torn in body, could walk no further. Shall he cast the walking stick aside? Not at all! Though he can walk no further, Jacob passes from this life to eternity leaning and resting on the precious old *staff.* This scripture in Hebrews refers back to Genesis 47:31, where Jacob in his old age, while still dwelling in Egypt, was facing death. He called his son Joseph and asked him to promise that he would not bury him in Egypt, but carry his body back to his homeland of Canaan. Verse 31 reads:

> *And he said, Swear unto me. And he swore unto him. And Israel (Jacob) bowed himself upon the bed's head.*

Listen very carefully, why is Genesis 47:31 translated as Jacob leaning on the "head of the bed" whereas Hebrews 11:21 is translated as Jacob leaning on "the head of the *staff?*" Don't miss this very significant point. As Gleason L. Archer states in the *Encyclopedia of Bible Difficulties*:

> "The Hebrew word for *staff* is *matteh* which is the same Hebrew word for *bed.* The word for bed and the word for *staff* are spelled exactly the same in the Hebrew consonants; only the vowel points

(first invented about the eighth century A.D. or a little before) differentiate between the two. But the Septuagint (the Greek translation of the Old Testament) translated back in the third century B.C. reads *m-t-h* as *mattah* (*staff*); it was the medieval Jewish Masoretes of the ninth century A.D. who decided it was *mittah* (bed). Hebrews 11:21 follows earlier vocalization and comes out with the far more likely rendering 'on the head of the *staff*' like the Septuagint and the Syriac Peshitta."[1]

The point I wish to make is that the word *mittah* (*staff*) is also the Hebrew word for bed, and as we view the Old Testament *staff* as a type of the Holy Spirit, is not He also our bed? We are called to rest in Him, to cast our every care upon Him, and allow Him to sustain our whole weight. The entire book of Hebrews speaks of believers finding their spiritual rest, for as we read in Hebrews 4:9,10:

> *There remaineth, therefore, a rest to the people of God.*
> *For he that is entered into his rest, he also hath ceased*
> *from his own works, as God did from his.*

What a beautiful insight when we realize that the words *staff* and bed are the very same word in the Hebrew language!

Let me digress a little bit and look at the book of Hebrews. The book was written to the 1st century Jewish Christians to confirm that Old Testament Judaism had come to an end through the work of Christ. The key word in the epistle is the word *better*, and the writer proceeds to show a series of contrasts between the Old Testament system of Judaism and the better things in Christ. One of these contrasts is to show the better rest we now have in the Holy Spirit. Listen to the words of Hebrews 3:7-11:

> *Wherefore, as the Holy Spirit saith, Today if you will hear his voice, Harden not your hearts, as in the provocation, in the day of trial in the wilderness, When your fathers put me to the test, proved me, and saw my works forty years. Wherefore, I was grieved with that generation, and said, They do always err in their heart, and they have not known my ways. So I swore in my wrath, they shall not enter into my rest.*

Repeatedly, God warned these Jewish Christians that their fathers who did not enter Canaan's land because of unbelief had no rest. They wandered in the desert for forty years in a state of constant turmoil and unrest. And likewise today, if we will find rest, it will be when we cease from self-effort and rely completely upon the Holy Spirit.

He is our bed and our *staff*, a resting place where we may rest our complete weight on Him. Entering into Canaan has always been viewed as a type of the believer's entering into the abundant spirit-filled rest. The only entrance into Canaan land is by way of the Spirit. Flesh alone can never carry us into this blessed land; we must be transported by the *staff* of the Spirit. I say without apology that salvation is a work of God, not an effort of man. What a beautiful truth to know that my relationship with God is a *resting* not a *wrestling*!

The Holy Spirit is our "Comforter" and in Him we may rest our full weight and struggle no more. The believer's service is no longer of self-effort, or a labor in the flesh, but rather a sweet rest in the Spirit's power, which can carry us from one victory to another.

> *(It's) Not by might, nor by power, but by my Spirit, saith the Lord of hosts* (Zechariah 4:6).

In the Holy Spirit believers do not have to perform, attain, or work to make it through life's journey, we simply "lean on the *staff*." And don't miss this, as Jacob was in Egypt (a type of the world) he longed to be buried in Canaan's fair land and by resting on the "head of the *staff*" he was carried safely home.

Moses

And the Lord said unto him, "What is that
in your hand?" And he said, "A rod."
                                                    Exodus 4:2

Recall, if you will, the story of Moses in Egypt. He had all the stuff, but no *staff*. There in Egypt he lived in ease and prosperity, as the son of Pharaoh's daughter. Physically, he was a striking specimen of humanity, standing head and shoulders above other men.

In the Old Testament account of his birth, we read that "he was beautiful" (Exodus 2:2). He was also very intelligent, for it is recorded in Acts 7:22 that he *was learned in all the wisdom of the Egyptians*. He was a true scholar in his day. We also read in Acts 7:22 that *he was mighty in words and in deeds*. In other words, he was a powerful leader, as well as a man of action and authority, who according to tradition was appointed general over the Egyptian army. However, he was not exactly a prime candidate for God's service. His hands were so filled with worldly goods that he had no room to hold a *staff*. You see, God cannot use a man with full hands. He desires men who can come to Him with empty hands that He might fill them.

God does not normally call a man who has all the world's wisdom, riches, intelligence and power. He wants a man who has nothing to offer, so that there is no room for that man to glory himself.

The life of Moses is an interesting one. Moses spent the

first forty years of his life building and preparing himself in a worldly way. God took the next forty years to perfect in Moses what would be essential for His service. He had to send Moses to the school of the wilderness to strip him of every earthly possession, position, passion, perspective, and prideful thought before he could be God's chosen vessel to deliver Israel from Egypt.

In Exodus 2 we read of the impetuous action of Moses in killing the Egyptian. Through this action came rejection on all sides. First by his own people, Israel; second, by the Egyptians; and finally by Pharaoh himself.

Moses had no choice. His kingdom literally crumbled around him. He had to run, and run he did! We read in Exodus 2:15 that when Pharaoh heard of this matter he tried to kill Moses. However, Moses fled from the presence of Pharaoh and settled in the land of Midian.

God started a forty-year process of demoting the would-be king to the position of a servant. Moses was led to the wilderness where he became a common shepherd, and learned to trod the desert sands until his skin was burned and his hair bleached with the desert sun. Moses exchanged his palace for desert sands; fountains of wine for a mountain stream; and his scepter for a shepherd's *staff*.

For forty years, Moses lived a quiet and reclusive life far from the sumptuous splendor of the king's table, riding in the king's chariot and commanding the king's army. Yes, Moses had a problem. He had suffered severe emotional disturbance. He was a marked man; his self-image was gone and self-confidence lost. He had lost it all! He finally was ready to graduate from the school of the Holy Spirit. And now, into the hands of this bewildered, frail, defeated, eighty-year-old man, God placed His graduation diploma, a *staff*.

From the burning bush on the side of the mountain, God called Moses to go back to Egypt and lead His people out of bondage. No, God was not through with Moses. He had only rehabilitated him for His service. Exodus 3:1-5 records the intriguing account of how God, through a supernatural process, rebuilt Moses' life. What took a lifetime to empty out, God filled in a moment. God spoke to him and asked, *What is that in thine hand?* Moses replied, *A rod!* (Exodus 4:2).

I believe, at this point, Moses was a little facetious. He probably thought, "God, now you call on me! There was a time I had everything to offer. Once, I had power and money. I was able to speak eloquently. But Lord, after forty years of tending sheep and talking to flea-bitten beasts, I've lost all my poise and dignity. Now you ask me what I have in my hand? Well, here it is! This ole shepherd's crook. Just this old stick! What's in my hand Lord? Nothing, except a *staff* only!"

Moses was about to learn a lesson he'd never forget, a lesson which took forty years of preparation. God was about to demonstrate to Moses the power in the *staff*. The rod was a sign of the power of God:

> *The Lord shall send the rod of thy strength out of Zion; rule thou in the midst of thine enemies* (Psalms 110:2).

Moses never knew power until he laid Pharaoh's scepter aside and laid hold on the *rod of God*. In Exodus 4:3, God told Moses to cast down the rod, or *staff*. When Moses obeyed, it became a serpent, and he fled from before it. Then, in verse 4, the Lord said to Moses:

> *Put forth thine hand, and take it by the tail. And he put forth his hand, and caught it, and it became a rod (staff) in his hand.*

I believe there is something here that we must notice.

Moses had to determine what he wished to do with the *staff* in his hand. Held securely, it would be the rod of power for the deliverance of Israel from the land of captivity. It was the means of Israel's salvation and deliverance from evil. When cast down, the *staff* became a vicious snake. The serpent, or snake, has always been a picture of Satan; the curse of sin, destruction and evil.

In life, we have the opportunity to take the *staff* of God in hand and perform the great works of God. If we reject God's way and cast down His *staff*, we open the door to evil and destruction. Moses fled from the serpent when he cast down the rod and, likewise, many who reject God's ways spend their lives on the run, being chased by the devil's little imps. If you cast down God's *staff*, it will be your undoing. Satan will chase you the rest of your life. You'll never experience victory, having cast down the precious, anointed *staff* of God.

Moses, by faith, reached down and picked up that snake by the tail, and it became the power of God, which was used throughout the rest of Moses' life.

Believe me, Moses never cast it down again unless it was to show the power of God. He held firmly to the *staff* for the remainder of his days. Moses is seen setting out with the *staff* in hand in Exodus 4:20:

> *And Moses took his wife and his sons, and set them upon an ass, and he returned to the land of Egypt; and Moses took the rod (**staff**) of God in his hand.*

He made his return to Egypt with a *staff*. God had instructed him in Exodus 4:17:

> *And thou shalt take this rod in thine hand, wherewith thou shalt do signs.*

It was the *staff* that Moses used to perform the miracles before Pharaoh that compelled him to let Israel go. It was the rod that turned into a serpent before the eyes of Pharaoh. It was the rod that turned the rivers of Egypt into blood (Exodus 7: 9, 17, 19, 20). It was the rod that was stretched over the rivers and ponds of Egypt to bring a plague of frogs upon all the land. It was the rod that stretched out to smite the land of Egypt with the plague of lice (Exodus 8:16). It was the rod of God that Moses stretched toward heaven, and the hailstones fell on Egypt (Exodus 9:23). It was the rod that brought the plague of locusts (Exodus 10:13). It was the rod that parted the water of the Red Sea and gave the children of Israel access to cross over to Sinai on dry ground. Exodus 14:16 says:

> But lift thou up thy rod, and stretch out thine hand over the sea, and divide it; and the children of Israel shall go on dry ground through the midst of the sea.

It was the rod that brought the water from the rock in the wilderness in Exodus 17:6:

> Behold, I stand before thee there upon the rock in Horeb; and thou shalt smite the rock, and there shall come water out of it, that the people may drink . . .

Also in Numbers 21:17,18 Israel was directed to the wells of water in the desert by the use of staves (*staffs*). It is recorded:

> Then Israel sang this song, Spring up, O well; sing ye unto it: The princes digged the well, the nobles of the people digged it, by the direction of the lawgiver, with their staves . . .

Dear friend, if we are to find the rivers of living water today, it will be through the *Staff of the Spirit*. In John 4:14 Jesus promised:

> But the water that I shall give him shall be in him a well of water springing up into everlasting life.

There's an abundant supply of "Living Water" for you, but it can only be found through the *staff*.

It was the rod that was held by Moses on the mountaintop that caused Israel to prevail over the Amalekites in Exodus 17:9.

> *And Moses said unto Joshua, choose us out men, and go out, fight with Amalek: tomorrow I will stand on the top of the hill with the rod of God in mine hand.*

Finally, we observe in Numbers 21:5-9 a most unusual use of the *staff* by Moses. The account unfolds with verse 7 as Israel faces a very frightful predicament. Because of their constant murmuring against God and Moses, the Lord sent fiery serpents among the people. These poisonous snakes were biting the people, and consequently many of the people were dying. God offered a solution. He told Moses to make a bronze serpent and put it on a pole. God further instructed Moses to have the people look upon the bronze serpent on the pole and they would be healed. I'm sure you have read and heard many sermons on the spiritual application of the bronze serpent and how the serpent was a symbol of sin and bronze a symbol of judgment. The bronze serpent has also been equated with Christ who was made sin for us and placed upon the cross to die for our sins. As we look up to Him, He offers spiritual healing and forgiveness of our sins, and we shall not experience death. But could there also be a type of the Holy Spirit in this as well?

As I considered the word "pole" for that upon which Moses placed the bronze serpent, I found it to mean simply a handheld stick or portable standard on which a flag may be carried into battle. Moses made a bronze serpent, fastened it to his *staff* or rod, and held it before the people to look to for healing. The spiritual application is obvious: the stick held up or supported the bronze serpent. If Christ will be lifted up, it will be through the Holy Spirit.

And, as Moses lifted up the serpent in the wilderness, even so must the Son of man be lifted up (John 3:14).

And I, if I be lifted up from the earth, will draw all men unto me (John 12:32).

Nevertheless, when he, the Spirit of truth, is come, he will guide you into all truth; for he shall not speak of himself, but whatever he shall hear, that shall he speak . . .
                                                    John 16:13

The Holy Spirit is come to glorify and exalt Jesus Christ and his work on the cross. Moses could not lift up the bronze serpent without a *staff* or standard. So, also, Christ will not be lifted up or exalted by the arm of flesh. There is not a preacher, evangelist, singer, choir, or church that can exalt Christ without a *staff* or standard of the Holy Spirit.

It is the present day ministry of the Holy Spirit to place Christ on display before men. The *staff* of the Spirit will raise up Christ in full view of men that they might look to Jesus and live. Christ will be lifted up by no other means, save the *staff.*

It can clearly be seen that Moses found an indispensable tool when he realized the power of the *staff.* It was a demonstration of God's miraculous power to the heathen nations. It parted the waters and made a way to escape the world. It brought fresh water to a thirsty people and victory to God's people over the enemy.

That's exactly what the Holy Spirit continues to do today! In retrospect, "Moses, what's that in thine hand? Just an old stick?" "No! Thank you, Lord, for taking from me the stuff of Egypt and giving me the *staff* of God."

The Children Of Israel's Exodus

And thus shall ye eat it: with your loins girded,
your shoes on your feet, and your staff in your hand;
and ye shall eat it in haste: it is the Lord's passover.

Exodus 12:11

There is no record in the Old Testament that paints a more vivid picture, or type, of the redemptive work of Christ, than the book of Exodus. Exodus, which means "exit" or "departure," is a fitting title for that which describes the going out of the chosen people from the land where they were held in bondage and slavery for generations.

Exodus is filled with precious types of Christ and his spiritual work of salvation in the heart of the believer. It presents such rich symbolic meanings in the Passover, manna, Egypt, the rock, the tabernacle, and Moses himself. I must not attempt to delve too deeply into this rich gold mine of types, for that would be a book in itself. I would like, however, to share a brief background for the verse of Scripture to which I am about to make reference.

God was at work in the lives of His children, Israel, who were held bondage in the land of Egypt. Pharaoh had resisted God as long as he could. The plagues were increasing with such intensity that Pharaoh finally consented to let the people of Israel go.

The plague that would break Pharaoh's stubborn will was the death of the first born in Egypt. God provided a way for Israel to be protected from this plague of death: it was the Passover. In Exodus 12, we have the account of the sacrifice of the Passover Lamb. The blood was shed and applied to the doorpost of each house wherein the families of Israel dwelt. They were instructed to gather all their household under one roof and eat the flesh of the

sacrificed lamb—and be ready for travel, for they were to
leave in haste at God's command.

> *And thus shall ye eat it: with your loins girded, your*
> *shoes on your feet, and your **staff** in your hand; and ye*
> *shall eat it in haste: it is the Lord's passover* (Exodus 12:11).

Not only is Christ and His sacrifice as our Passover Lamb
portrayed in the Old Testament book of Exodus; but there
also appears the *staff.*

Consequently, the Holy Spirit is once again typified as
the walking stick (take nothing for your journey, save a
staff). Israel was instructed to take their journey from the
land of Egypt with *staff* in hand. Christian, when we are
called out of this world, released from the bondage of sin,
we are also instructed to take the *staff* in hand. We will
never make the journey to separate ourselves from the world
without the power of the Holy Spirit. And yet, Christians
foolishly endeavor to make the great escape solely on foot:
the foot of flesh. How obtuse and preposterous! It's like
trying to fly without a plane, or cross the Atlantic without
a ship, or climb the Swiss Alps without a rope, or dig your
way to China with a teaspoon. When will Christians realize
that the deliverance from the things of the world demands
the use of the *Staff of the Spirit?*

I have been pastoring God's people for nearly twenty
years, and I see such frustration in their lives. Christians
feel that because they have applied the blood of the Passover
Lamb, Jesus, to their lives that they are automatically
delivered from the bondage of sin and slavery.

I believe that deliverance will not come until we secure
the *staff.* Paul the apostle came to this realization in Romans
7 and 8. He is held in the frustrating grips of sin in chapter
7, verses 15-18:

> *For that which I do I understand not; for what I would, that do I not; but what I hate, that do I. If, then, I do that which I would not, I consent unto the law that it is good. Now, then, it is no more I that do it, but sin that dwelleth in me. For I know that in me (that is, in my flesh) dwelleth no good thing; for to will is present with me, but how to perform that which is good I find not.*
>
> *Oh, wretched man that I am! Who shall deliver me from the body of this death* (Romans 7:24)?

This sounds like many of those I counsel, who are held in the bondage of sin. However, Paul knew the answer: he caught hold of the *staff* and never let go. Yes, in chapter 8 of Romans Paul finalizes it. Victory comes by way of the Spirit. There will be a conflict, just as there was a conflict in Egypt as Pharaoh and his armies pursued after Israel— but he didn't catch them! The flesh will pursue after the Spirit, but God will part the waters for you. The flesh does not stand a chance when we're walking with the *staff* in hand. My Christian friend, don't leave Egypt without it!

It is interesting to note in Exodus 12:11 that the *staff* was placed in the hands of the children of Israel at the time of the Passover. Verse 7 says:

> *And they shall take of the blood, and strike it on the two side posts . . .*
>
> *And thus shall ye eat it: with your loins girded, your shoes on your feet, and **your staff** in your hand . . .* (Exodus 12:11).

When the blood was applied in the land of bondage, the *staff* was also given.

Since the *staff* is an Old Testament type of the Holy Spirit, the lamb a type of Christ's shed blood at Calvary, and Egypt a type of the world and sin, then it would only be logical to conclude that a person who is saved by the blood and released from the bondage of sin, also receives the Holy Spirit at salvation.

As stated earlier, there are some who would advocate the view that a Christian must seek to receive the Holy Spirit, as a subsequent work of grace, later in their Christian walk. I believe there are many works of grace in the Christian life, and also many works of faith. However, believers receive all the necessary tools, or spiritual equipment, for their walk, or journey of life, at salvation. Although, it is up to them to exercise these spiritual graces on a daily basis.

Israel had a long journey from Egypt to Canaan, and the only way they could successfully move ahead was through the use of the *staff*. They stepped out by faith!

Although many believers today hold the *Staff of the Spirit* in hand, they know nothing of its power. They wander through the wilderness of sin and defeat, never appropriating the *Staff of the Spirit* that enables them to cross the spiritual Jordan into the abundant Christian life.

The activities of Israelites in their wilderness wanderings portray what many of us see in our churches today: doubt, fear, unbelief, murmuring, rebellion against spiritual leadership, carnality, and a multitude of other fleshly manifestations. It was a relatively short journey from Egypt to Canaan, but it took Israel forty years to get there. They were *under the blood* (salvation), and *went through the waters* (baptism), but were not *in the Spirit.* Oh, Christian, *Are ye so foolish? Having begun in the Spirit, are ye now made perfect by the flesh* (Galatians 3:3)?

If Christians would stop fussing about when you get it, how you get it, and who gets it, and by simple faith exercise it, we would see victory and power as we have never seen since Pentecost.

May I add a small side note that might clarify something that is likely to raise some eyebrows? When I say "it," I refer to the power, not the person. I am very aware that the *staff* is a "He" and not an "it." The Holy Spirit is the Third Person of the Godhead, and it is He of whom I speak.

For too long we have disputed with one another over terms. One camp is so avid in their emphasis of the Spirit that they idolize the Spirit. The other camp is so opposed to the emphasis of the Spirit that they grieve the Spirit. The pendulum swings from one extreme to the other and never seems to strike a balance. Truth out of balance will always produce error. Jesus set the balance well when He said in John 4:24:

> *God is a Spirit; and they that worship him must worship him in spirit and in truth.*

Truth without spirit is dead and boring; it will kill.

> *Who also hath made us able ministers of the new testament, not of the letter, but of the spirit; for the letter killeth, but the Spirit giveth life* (2 Corinthians 3:6).

The Spirit, without truth, is chaotic and erroneous, and will quickly lead to division, strife, and vainglory.

Many Christians long to see some life and freshness in the church. Oh, they hear the Word of God, as it's preached, taught, dissected, expounded, and resounded, but there is no true worship, praise, or power. On the other hand, there are those that are weary of the emotional, eruptive services, where freedom of worship leads to outbursts of carnal demonstrations. They long for some structure, organization, and leadership, and they hunger for the truth of the Word. Something is missing when their worship gets "carried away" to the point where there is no time for the preacher, no time to be fed, and no time for the truth.

I have discovered that God's people, His Church, are desperately crying out for balance. They long for a Moses to deliver them from sin and bondage, and for a Joshua who will lead them into the abundant Christian life. You see, Moses was a great deliverer but he could not lead the children of Israel into the Promised Land. He led them through the blood and through the water, but could not lead them in the Spirit. God had to raise up a Joshua to finally lead Israel across the Jordan and into the land of spiritual conquest. We need more Joshuas today!

[1] Taken from the book, *Encyclopedia Of Bible Difficulties* by Gleason L. Archer, Copyright ©1982 by Zondervan Corporation, Zondervan Publishing House, Grand Rapids. Used by permission.

THE STAFF AND THE SPIRIT [1]

Let's compare in the scriptures, both the Old and the New,
  what the *staff* and the Spirit mean to you.
They seem like they're different and yet they're the same,
  used by God for His glory so that man He could gain.

Jacob lied and he schemed, and was a deceitful man,
  until God with a *staff* brought forth His new plan.
If your life's like Jacob's, you'll reap what you've sown,
  let the Spirit take over and your life He will own.

Moses lived in a palace, rode a chariot of the king,
  God emptied his hands so to the *staff* he would cling.
Are we searching for riches, for glory and fame?
  Holy Spirit take it all until we're never the same.

Many miracles were wrought with the *staff* we are told,
  as the Children of Israel stood before the Pharoah of old.
The Spirit's still moving and God's answering prayer
  to deliver us all from the Enemy's snare.

With *staff* in his hand Gideon won a great war,
  though his army was few and the enemy more.
We're never outnumbered with God on our side,
  any battle can be won when the Spirit is our guide!

Goliath stood tall and at David he would laugh,
    but David prevailed with his sling and his *staff*.
Do trials and temptations seem awesome and great?
    With the Spirit within us we're free of all hate.

The spies came back with gripes on their tongues,
    yet the grapes were so big, on a *staff* they were hung.
For us today there's a Canaan land too,
    let the fruit of the Spirit grow abundantly in you.

Joshua with *staff* went willingly out,
    the victory was won by a trump and a shout.
The strongholds around us will crumble and fall,
    just yield to the Spirit and heed to His call.

Do you feel you're not worthy like these men of old?
    It was the *staff* in their hands that made them so bold.
Let the Spirit take over and have His own way,
    and you'll find new victories, it can happen today.

The men of old with *staff* in their hand,
    used it for instruction and authority to command.
Today the Spirit indwells in our heart
    to fill us, anoint us, and His power impart.

The shepherd with *staff* watched over his sheep,
    he'd protect them and lovingly see to their keep.
The Spirit will convict us and reveal to us sin,
    and warn us when the Enemy will try to come in.

Are you concerned about family not yet under the blood,
    whom the cares of this world overtake like a flood?
The *staff* was used for lost sheep gone astray,
    Holy Spirit draw our loved ones to the Cross this day.

Have you lost your anointing, and there's blessings no more,
    and the curse of Ichabod is written on your door?
Take the *staff* in your hand and you'll surely see
    that the Spirit-filled life will bring victory for thee!

Nancy Lewis

[1] *The Staff And The Spirit* by Nancy Lewis, Copyright © 1990

chapter 5

God's Men On Staff

Part II

Gideon

Then the angel of the Lord put forth the end of the staff that was in his hand, and touched the flesh and the unleavened cakes; and there rose up fire out of the rock . . .

Judges 6:21

Israel was in trouble once again, as the Midianites held them captive for seven years. It was now God's purpose that Israel be set free from the oppression of the enemy, so God looked for a man. God could do the work himself, but I'm so glad He chooses men to do His bidding. God certainly does not need the help of men. He could simply do everything himself, but He has chosen to use human vessels.

*And I sought for a man among them, that should make
up the hedge, and stand in the gap before me for the land,
that I should not destroy it; but I found none* (Ezekiel
22:30).

God does not bless organizations, networks, churches,
denominations, or even nations. He blesses individual men.
God works through men! God will bless organizations,
networks, churches, denominations, and nations, through
a man.

Does God look for men big enough to work through?
No, God's not looking for mighty men, wise men, or noble
men; but rather the foolish, the weak, and the despised.
God longs for empty men, vessels that are not full, but
empty and simply available. Men whose hands are full of
mundane resources will not have room to hold a *staff.*

*For ye see your calling, brethren, how that not many
wise men after the flesh, not many mighty, not many noble,
are called; But God hath chosen the foolish things of the
world to confound the wise; and God hath chosen the
weak things of the world to confound the things which
are mighty; And base things of the world, and things which
are not, to bring to nothing things that are, That no flesh
should glory in his presence* (1 Corinthians 1:26-29).

What was Gideon's response to the call of God when
God said, "Gideon, you will be my instrument to deliver
Israel from the hand of the Midianites?"

*Lord, wherewith shall I save Israel? Behold, my family
is poor in Manasseh, and I am the least in my father's
house* (Judges 6:15).

We might reconstruct their dialogue like this:

Here, Gideon, take this stick!

Gideon must have replied, "A stick? Sure Lord, you want
me to beat off a million and one Midianites with a stick!"

Aye, but Gideon you don't know what's in that stick.

It's the *Staff of the Spirit!*

Judges 6:21 says:

> *Then the angel of the Lord put forth the end of the staff that was in his hand, and touched the flesh and the unleavened cakes; and there rose up fire out of the rock, and consumed the flesh and the unleavened cakes. Then the angel of the Lord departed out of his sight.*

It's like God said to Gideon, "Here son, let me show you how it works."

I am not going into further detail on what happened after that, but let me refresh your memory on how God wrought a great victory through a man with a *Staff* in hand. Recall, if you will, how God told Gideon that the army of Israel had too many soldiers. Gideon started with 32,000 and God reduced the army to 300. In Judges 7:2 the Lord said:

> *The people who are with thee are too many for me to give the Midianites into their hands, lest Israel vaunt themselves against me, saying, Mine own hand hath saved me.*

God finally reduced the army of Israel to 300 men without a conventional weapon, and sent them to the camp of the Midianites. Verse 12 says:

> *The Midianites and the Amalekites and all the children of the east lay along in the valley like grasshoppers for multitude; and their camels were without number, as the sand by the seaside for multitude.*

These are not very good odds for a group of 300 men, each carrying a trumpet, a lamp, and a pitcher; but, who needs warriors and weapons when you have God's "walking stick?" I'd take the *staff* anytime, wouldn't you?

When will we ever comprehend that our greatest weapon and protection against the enemy is the Spirit of God? The odds are against us in the spiritual warfare if we rely solely on our flesh. We have no power to stand against *principalities,*

*evil powers, rulers of this dark world, and spiritual wickedness
in high places* (Ephesians 6:12). This is not a battle for
flesh and blood; it is one that demands a *staff.*

Oh, that we might depend upon the Spirit of God for
our protection and defense. The shepherd's *staff* was the
main tool of defense along the rough wilderness terrain
of the Middle East. If wild beasts would threaten the
vulnerable flock, the shepherd would quickly drive them
away, with a prodding, piercing *staff.* In the Shepherd's
Psalm, 23:4, we read:

> *Yea, though I walk through the valley of the shadow
> of death, I will fear no evil; for thou art with me; thy
> rod and thy staff they comfort me.*

What harm can befall us, or what savage, devilish beast
can overtake us if we but hold securely to our *staff?*

Once again, I urge my readers not to misconstrue my
strong emphasis on the Spirit. Truth out of balance becomes
error, and I certainly do not wish to misemploy the Scripture.
I am not advocating that we should do nothing to protect
or defend ourselves. There are certain precautions and
safeguards we must take in life. However, the material
substance that God has allowed us to possess must be
considered secondary and not primary, a means to an end
and not an end itself. In our case, for life and freedom,
I would urge that the best possible training and equipping
be sought—provided we do not regard these as ends in
themselves. While knowledge of weaponry may make men
feel strong and secure, it is only the *staff* that produces
real strength.

In Gideon's case, it was the *staff* that brought fire out
of the rock. Gideon took men with him, a deployment of
troops with other objects in their hands (trumpets, pitchers,
and lamps); but it was the *staff* that wrought the victory!

We, in America, must get back to faith in the living God, and lay hold on the *Staff of the Spirit.* In 2 Kings 19:14, we read that when Hezekiah, the king of Israel, received the threat of war from the Assyrian army, *he went up into the house of the Lord, and spread it before the Lord.*

Would to God, we would do that in America today. Thank you God for our defense program and for strong armies; but above all, God, give us a *staff.* Amen!

David

*And he took his **staff** in his hand, and chose five smooth stones out of the brook, and put them in a shepherd's bag which he had, even in a wallet; and his sling was in his hand: and he drew near the Philistine.*
1 Samuel 17:40

David was much different from Moses in that he had nothing for God to strip away. David was but a youth, a lowly shepherd boy, the youngest of eight sons of Jesse.

And David rose up early in the morning, and left the sheep with a keeper, and took, and went, as Jesse had commanded him (1 Samuel 17:20).

David was an errand boy sent by his father to take food to the three eldest boys who were members of Saul's army. When David arrived at the camp to deliver the food, he heard the words of Goliath, the giant of the Philistine army. He saw the reproach that this man was bringing on Israel, and his defiance of the armies of the living God.

David boldly spoke up and said he alone would go against this blasphemous giant. Of course, David's older brothers were angry when they heard David say this. I would paraphrase their sarcastic remarks as, "David, go back and feed your scant little herd of sheep. You're no soldier!"

When Saul, the king of Israel, heard of David's offer,
he sent for him to come. He was desperate, and willing
to try anything. David testified that he knew that God was
with him and that God would empower him to silence the
belligerent enemy of Israel. In verse 37, David said:

> *Moreover, The Lord who delivered me out of the paw
> of the lion, and out of the paw of the bear, he will deliver
> me out of the hand of the Philistine.*

David was convinced that all God needed was a willing
vessel. Saul was certainly not as convinced of the power
of God as David was. His only reply was, *Go, and the Lord
be with thee* (1 Samuel 17:37).

Saul tried to arm David by placing his armor and helmet
on the young boy. He loaded David down with the
"essentials" for battle: armor, shield, helmet, coat of mail,
and a sword; all the paraphernalia that the world deems
necessary. I especially like verse 39: *And David put them
off.* Praise God! David knew what was necessary. I can
imagine David saying, "No offense, Saul, but keep your
junk—just give me my *staff!*"

> *And he took his **staff** in his hand (take nothing for your
> journey, except a **staff**) and chose five smooth stones out
> of the brook, and put them in a shepherd's bag which
> he had, even in a wallet; and his sling was in his hand:
> and he drew near the Philistine* (1 Samuel 17:40).

When the Philistine looked at David he could not believe
his eyes. He must have thought to himself, "This is but
a youth." I'm amused when I read the Philistine's response
in verse 43 and imagine him saying, "What do you think
you are coming out here to kill, a dog? All you have is
a slingshot and that simple little stick in your hand."

What the poor giant didn't realize was that simple little
stick represented the power and presence of Almighty God

who rules the universe. David responded with, "Thou comest to me with a sword, and with a spear, and with a shield; but I come to thee in the name of the Lord of Hosts, the God of the armies of Israel." Needless to say, the giant and all the armies of the Philistines knew that day there was a God in heaven; for Goliath had met his match. One small stone from David's sling went straightway into the forehead of Goliath. David had smote the Philistine, and the world's champion was dead.

You can have your rockets, atomic bombs, fighter jets, tanks, and nuclear war heads. I'll take God's **staff** any day!

Benaiah

And he slew an Egyptian, a handsome man, and the Egyptian had a spear in his hand; but he went down to him with a staff, and plucked the spear out of the Egyptian's hand, and slew him with his own spear.
2 Samuel 23:21 and 1 Chronicles 11:23

I love to read the biblical accounts of mighty men of valor and their heroic deeds. David's mighty men have always especially fascinated me. Adino, the chief of the captain, lifted up his spear against eight-hundred strong at one time, and slew them all. Eleazar, the son of Dodo, rose up and smote the Philistines until his hand adhered to the sword. Shammah, who saw the Philistines gathered together into a troop where there was a plot and defended it until he slew all the Philistines; and the Lord wrought a great victory.

One valiant man particularly stands out in my mind. His name is Benaiah. His mighty deed is recorded in 1 Chronicles 11:23,24. Verse 23 states:

And he slew an Egyptian, a man of great stature, five cubits tall; and in the Egyptian's hand was a spear like *a weaver's beam; and he went down to him with a **staff**, and plucked the spear out of the Egyptian's hand, and slew him with his own spear.*

What a contrast in weaponry! One combatant armed with a spear the size of a weaver's beam, the other with a *staff* the size of a broom handle. That's like going after a grizzly bear with a hickory switch. But, beloved, give me that hickory stick with the power of God in it and watch what happens!

The Spies In Canaan
(Grapes or Gripes?)

*And they came unto the brook of Eshcol, and cut down from there a branch with one cluster of grapes, and they bore it between two upon a **staff**.*

Numbers 13:23

One of the most delightful scriptures which emphasizes the blessings of God upon His people is found in Numbers 13:17-25. I love to preach from this text and dramatize how the twelve spies were sent from the wilderness of Paran to spy out the land of Canaan. They were instructed to go up into the mountain to see what God had prepared for them: to view and foretaste the good things that were waiting for them on the other side of Jordan. Not only would they see the land and its plentiful fruit, but they would get a glimpse of their opposition as well. They realized they had to drive out the inhabitants of Canaan and overthrow their cities and strongholds. The result would be a multitude of God's blessings upon them.

Numbers 13:18-20 states:

And see the land, what it is; and the people who dwell therein, whether they are strong or weak, few or many;

And what the land is that they dwell in, whether it is good or bad; and what cities they are that they dwell in, whether in camps, or in strong-holds; and what the land is, whether fat or lean, whether there is wood therein, or not. And be ye of good courage, and bring of the fruit of the land.

I believe Canaan is a type—an example of the kind of dwelling place God desires for all believers. It is the land of abundant life where the spiritual air is pure, refreshing waters flow, and the fruit of blessings abound. It is a place of spiritual victory where the enemy is defeated and daily conquest enjoyed. Yes, there are giants to overcome, great walled cities to march around, and mountains to climb; but, as we submit to our Joshua (Jesus), we may be *more than conquerors.* This is the *land that flows with milk and honey.* It's called the abundant, spirit-filled, Christian life— the place where every believer should desire to dwell.

I realize, that, even as I write, there are many Christians who have never visited this land to taste of the fruit therein, nor have they viewed the beautiful green valleys from Mount Pisgah's lofty heights, nor drunk from the refreshing springs of Negev; nor have they felt the surge of spiritual power.

I wish I could say that I personally have found a permanent residence there and that I have experienced all that God intends for the believer to enjoy. However, perhaps at least God has called me to be a spy—to spy out the land and return with a report of its magnificent spiritual wealth. Yes, I can honestly say I've been there! I thank God that he has enabled me, and I pray that by His grace He will continue to enable me to present to others a taste of the blessed fruit of Canaan.

It is recorded in verse 20 of this same chapter that the spies were in Canaan at the time of the first harvesting of grapes. Verse 23 says:

*And they came unto the brook of Eshcol, and cut down
from there a branch with one cluster of grapes, and they
bore it between two **upon a staff**.*

Can you imagine the joy and delight to be permitted
to enter the camp of the children of Israel with such a
manifestation of God's riches? If the grapes were the size
of apples can you imagine how big the tomatoes,
cantaloupes, melons, and oranges must have been? Even
the grapes were not nearly as large as the Israelites' eyes
when they beheld such a wonder. Oh, dear friend, are you
amazed and filled with such excitement and wonder when
presented the blessed fruit of the Spirit? Is it possible to
catch a glimpse of what God has in store for all of His
children who enter into the abundant land of the spirit-
filled life?

When the Apostle Paul described Christian character in
Galatians 5:22-26, he used an analogy, calling it *the fruit
of the Spirit*. Do you stand in awe as Paul displays each
magnificent cluster of fruit—the fruit of *love, joy, peace,
longsuffering, gentleness, goodness, faith, meekness, and self-
control*? Do you see that each large cluster of fruit is borne
on a *staff*, the Holy Spirit? As the grapes of Eshcol were
borne between two *upon a staff*, so also is the fruit of
abundant Christian character borne upon the *Staff of the
Spirit*: an impossible task by one's own efforts. Dear
Christian, the flesh can never bear the load of the fruit
as described in Galatians, chapter five. We are incapable
of carrying the fruit of Canaan back for others to view
without the *staff*. Man, in the flesh, simply cannot sustain
such a burden.

Numbers 13:25 says that the spies returned after forty
days of searching out the land, and *showed them the fruit
of the land* (verse 26). Oh, but it does not end there: for

with every blessing there is a battle, with every mountain there is a valley, and with every rainbow there is a rainstorm. Verse 28 bears this out:

> *Nevertheless, the people are strong that dwell in the land, and the cities are walled, and very great: and, moreover, we saw the children of Anak (giants) there.*

Then they, just as many Christians do today, began to make excuses:

> *. . . We are not able to go up against the people; for they are stronger than we . . . The land, through which we have gone to search it, is a land that eateth up the inhabitants thereof; and all the people that we saw in it are of great stature. And there we saw the giants, the sons of Anak, . . . and we were in our own sight as grasshoppers, and so we were in their sight* (Numbers 13:31-33).

Contrasted by the delight of the "giant fruit" is the scorn of the "giant men." Caleb stilled the people and said:

> *Let us go up at once, and possess it; for we are well able to overcome it* (verse 30).

Caleb was saying, in essence, that the *staff* which carried the blessing of the giant fruit to you, will also carry the giant men away from you.

Continue to trust the *staff!* It has brought you this far, and it will carry you through Canaan! May I remind you of the words of Paul:

> *There hath no temptation taken you but such as is common to man; but God is faithful, who will not permit you to be tempted above that ye are able, but will, with the temptation, also make the way to escape, that ye may be able to bear it* (1 Corinthians 10:13).

Dear child of God, trust the precious *staff* to give you victory in any situation and carry you safely through every trial.

Because of fear and unbelief, there are those who will
never enter the promised land *that flows with milk and honey.*
Any rational person would be delighted for a land that
offered nothing but blessed fruit and prosperity; but God
has chosen to allow giants to dwell in the same land. He
never promised blessings without battles, comfort without
conflicts, nor fruit without a fight. He did promise a *staff*
that would sustain us and the ability to overcome any
obstacle through His power. As Caleb said, "We are *well
able* to overcome it!"

Numbers 14:1-2 records the response of the children of
Israel:

> *And all the congregation lifted up their voice, and cried;
> and the people wept that night. And all the children of
> Israel murmured against Moses and against Aaron . . . .*

As a consequence of their continual griping against God
and Moses, they spent the next forty years wandering in
the desolate wilderness. In Numbers 14:29, 30 God said:

> *Your carcasses shall fall in this wilderness; and all who
> were numbered of you, . . . who have murmured against
> me, Doubtless ye shall not come into the land, ...*

God punished Israel with one year of toil for every day
the spies viewed the good things of Canaan. The spies had
beheld the beauty of Canaan for forty days. Now, as a
result, they would view the ugly desolation of the wilderness
for forty years. What a terrible price to pay for unbelief
and murmuring! They had chosen the *Gripes* instead of the
Grapes, and consequently paid a very costly price.

The price for the rejection of God's anointing is nothing
less today. Oh, the unbelief and murmuring heard today
against God and God's men, when the command is issued
to walk forth in the victorious life of the Spirit. Christians
seem very content to wander in the desert lands of sin and

self, continually murmuring about wanting the leeks and onions of Egypt. There will never be power in service nor victory over sin until Christians today are willing to exercise the same kind of leadership that was demonstrated by Caleb and Joshua, the only two individuals of the entire generation who had the faith in God to go over into the blessed land of spiritual Canaan. Are you camping in Canaan's land? Or are you teetering between the lands of Grapes and Gripes?

Aaron

And the Lord said unto Moses, Bring Aaron's rod again before the testimony, to be kept for a sign against the rebels; and thou shalt quite take away their murmurings from me, that they die not.
Numbers 17:10

God has a unique and unusual way of choosing those whom He calls to minister in the temple. Then, as now, people murmur against God's chosen men. Does this sound familiar? I sincerely believe that if there is a problem that plagues the church today it is the deadly evil of murmuring! The Israelites complained about everything; nothing seemed to satisfy them. They griped about their needs when they weren't met, and even when they were. They were dissatisfied with manna, complained of the water shortage, desired flesh or meat for food, despised Moses as their leader, and longed to be back in Egypt. The weather was uncooperative—it was either too hot or too cold; too wet or too dry. Their complaints were endless.

Consequently, in Numbers 11:1, God revealed His displeasure with them:

And when the people complained, it displeased the Lord: and the Lord heard it; and His anger was kindled; and the fire of the Lord burned among them, and consumed those who were in the farthest parts of the camp.

A visible sign of a Christian who is out of fellowship with the Lord is a complaining spirit. As grievous as this is to the heart of God, the greatest grief to the Lord is the complaining and murmuring against men of God whom He has called and anointed as leaders.

Numbers 16:3 states that Korah took a group of about 250 men who rose up against God's men and said:

. . . Ye take too much upon you, seeing all the congregation are holy, everyone of them, and the Lord is among them: wherefore, then, lift ye up yourselves above the congregation of the Lord?

Korah, before the whole congregation, challenged Moses' and Aaron's leadership by asking, "Lord, who's right?" the Bible says,

And it came to pass, as he had finished speaking all these words, that the ground split open that was under them; And the earth opened its mouth, and swallowed them up, and their houses, and all the men that appertained unto Korah, and all their goods. They, and all that appertained to them, went down alive into sheol, and the earth closed upon them and they perished from among the congregation (Numbers 16:31-33).

I can visualize, following God's judgment upon Korah and his followers, the remaining Israelites realization of God's wrath, followed by their confession of the sin of murmuring against God's annointed.

In order to avoid the necessity of ever having to repeat such a drastic measure, God chose another way of manifesting His favor upon His chosen leader, Aaron. Numbers 17:10 reads:

And the Lord said unto Moses, Bring Aaron's rod again before the testimony, to be kept for a sign against the rebels;

and thou shalt quite take away their murmurings from me, that they die not.

There was soon to be no question about God's selection as high priest over Israel. He had ordained a very special sign to rest upon His anointed priest. He instructed each of the twelve tribes of Israel to engrave their names upon each rod and bring them to the tabernacle of the congregation. May I say, at this point, that I do not believe that these rods were freshly cut sticks—for then the miraculous would not nearly be so obvious. To clarify this point, let me share with you a brief illustration. Recently, at the church I pastor, a youth pastor was called to work full-time with our college and teen ministries. We were so excited when Pastor Ken and Nancy accepted the call to join our pastoral staff. The church social committee planned a surprise welcome party for the couple on a Sunday evening with a cake, ice cream, and a money tree as a token of our love. To make provisions for the money tree, a branch was cut from a tree and placed in a pot of plaster of paris. The cash that was collected from the congregation was tied to the tree with ribbons, giving the appearance of a tree bearing money.

Ironically, this event was held in the early spring months before the trees had budded. Following the party, the cash was gleaned from the branches and Pastor Ken and Nancy decided it would be a nice gesture to take this small, dead tree and place it in their youth activity room and hang photos of the church youth from its branches.

Surprisingly, after about a week had passed, we noticed that this dead, lifeless branch of an apple tree had begun to blossom. Had a miracle taken place? Of course not. Even though this branch was cut off from a tree, it still contained enough life-producing sap to allow it to blossom. Needless to say, however, it soon withered and ceased to show signs of life. It did not bud and yield fruit. My firm belief is that the rods which were brought to Moses to be placed in the tabernacle of the congregation were not freshly cut sticks, but were dead, dry staves or *staffs*, empty of sap and lifeless. In reality, I believe that they were the personal *staffs* that each tribal leader had carried with him out of Egypt.

As the account continues, the twelve rods were then brought in and placed together in the tabernacle. On the following day, Moses entered the tabernacle and saw that Aaron's rod, or dry stick, had become a living branch. It was Aaron's rod which *was budded, and brought forth buds, and bloomed blossoms, and yielded almonds* (Numbers 17:8). God had chosen Aaron!

Interestingly, Aaron's rod could not be mistaken as a fraud, for the rod engraved with his name, yielded not only buds, but blossoms and fruit concurrently. The proof of God's anointing on an individual today is evidenced by the fact that what he accomplishes cannot be performed by flesh or physical strength, but only by the presence of the supernatural. It's impossible for the natural man to produce bud, blossom, and fruit all at once.

Many ministries today are empowered by man's expertise and ability, but fail to manifest the supernatural, miracle-working power of the Holy Spirit. There is no doubt in the hearts and minds of God's people when a true man of God stands before them—the supernatural power of God will be evidenced in his life.

Aaron's ministry was distinguishable from all others in that it manifested the blessings of God, and yielded an increase that could not be attributed to planting or watering by man.

I believe there are too many men in the ministry who are clutching a dead, dry, "lifeless" stick. There are no signs of fruitfulness or productivity in their ministries. Many of them are self-called, self-motivated, self-empowered preachers, preaching dead sermons to dead congregations. Where is the unction of the Holy Spirit today? The absence of tears of compassion, fiery sermons, and "budding rods" are indicators of the deadness of which I speak.

Ordination councils today are commissioning young men into the ministry on the merits of the number of volumes of theological writings in their libraries, the number of earned degrees following their names, or their display of intellect and oratorical ability. Are these boards at all concerned that a man bear a *staff* that has budded, blossomed, and yields fruit?

There are some who would have us believe that the anointing of God is on their lives. They temporarily bud forth, but there are no genuine blossoms, and no lasting fruit. Their ministries are devoid of the supernatural work of God. What little evidence of life is quickly gone, and the fruit does not remain.

I am reminded of Jesus' words in John 15:16:

> *Ye have not chosen me, but I have chosen you, and ordained you, that ye should go and bring forth fruit, and that your fruit should remain.*

Is the holy anointing of any importance at all? Do ministers today have the unction to funtion? If fruitfulness and life within the rod constitutes anointing for service, how do we know if our ministries are fulfilling God's purpose if we show lasting signs of life?

Numbers 17:8, as quoted previously, states that Aaron's rod *was budded, and brought forth buds, and bloomed blossoms, and yielded almonds.* Notice, it does not tell us how many buds, blossoms, or almonds. Numbers do not mean anointing, size does not constitute success, assets do not indicate anointing, and complexity of operation does not validate one's calling. Just because a minister has a fleet of buses, pastors 1,000 people, airs several radio and television programs, drives a Lincoln, and builds a large cathedral, it does not necessarily indicate the anointing of God.

The question that must be asked is not "How well is it working?" but rather "Who is working it?" We must not be deceived by numbers or size, because great things can be accomplished in the flesh. Remember the evidence that God's anointing was on Aaron was not the *amount* of almonds but the presence of buds, blossoms, and fruit.

If man alone is working the *staff*, at best, there will be temporary fruit; but if God is at work, the ministry will be evidenced by these three distinctives—buds, blossoms, and fruit that remain. First, the buds symbolize life. When I look at a tree in the springtime, I see an old, dry, brown stick that seems dead and lifeless. But the first sign of life is when buds break forth upon its branches. Likewise, the first sign of God's anointing is the new life from within manifested in an outward bud. To the preacher I would ask, "Is there life in your ministry? Does your preaching generate enthusiasm, joy, newness, and outward expression of life in your congregation?" Second, the blossoms symbolize sweet fragrance. Oh, how I remember so well the smell of springtime in the air growing up near Shucker's fruit orchard. The air was permeated with the sweet smell of apple and cherry blossoms—an unmistakable sign of spring. So our ministries must bear the fragrance and sweetness of the Holy Spirit. To preachers I would also ask, "Is there a constant sweetness and freshness to your ministry or have things gone sour while you live on stale, musty messages from God?" I believe that the anointing on God's men will produce a messenger who hears often from the Lord and receives new and fresh insights and revelations. The minister who must resort to old cliches, canned messages, and worn out phrases, and knows nothing more than what he can parrot from others, lacks anointing. Third, the fruit symbolizes the final product. *Wherefore, by their fruits ye shall know them* (Matthew 7:20). The bottom line is, what is the product of your ministry? I would address pastors by saying, "Our people are the product of our ministry. We cannot blame all the church problems on our congregation, but in reality our congregations are a mere reflection of our own spirituality. We can raise our people no higher than our own spiritual level. Give me one hour to fellowship with the flock and I'll tell you what kind of shepherd they have. What is the fruit of our labors? Simply put: To reproduce Jesus Christ in the lives of our people. The pastor sets the spiritual level of his church, and the fruit of his labors will not only be the conversion of souls but also the maturity and spiritual development of the body of Christ. His labors may not be in great volume, but his work will manifest life, freshness and the character of God in his flock. God is not impressed with explosive, flamboyant beginnings but with lasting eternal results!

Some of the most precious men of God, whom I know personally, are laboring faithfully in small parishes with ministries that are fruitful, edifying, and nurturing in discipleship. There's joy and peace among their flocks with a feeling of contentment, as their sheep are well fed from the fruit yielded through these men's lives. Their flocks are not complacent nor do they speak against their shepherds, for they recognize them as God's men. Their lives demonstrate the character of God, as they lovingly and firmly feed, comfort, and disciple their flocks while leading others to Jesus Christ. Their lives yield the fruit of love, joy, peace, longsuffering, gentleness, faith, meekness, and self-control. It is evident that what was once a dry, lifeless "stick," now abounds and flourishes with the fruitfulness of God. Oh, don't allow acitivities and works to become confused with anointing—there is a vast difference. The evidence of God's anointing on the man of God is not found in talent or ability. Nor is it found in education or methods of administration. The anointing is apparent when a man demonstrates to his people that God is supernaturally at work in his life, ever bearing spiritual fruit for God's glory.

I would like to make one final point before leaving the subject of Aaron and his budding rod. As God gave specific instructions to Moses to build the tabernacle in the wilderness, he instructed him to place three items inside the Ark of the Covenant. These three items would remain there as a token for all generations. In Hebrews 9:3,4 there is a listing of these specific items:

> And after the second veil, the tabernacle, which is called the Holiest of all, which had the golden censer, and the ark of the covenant overlaid round about with gold, in which was the golden pot that had manna, and Aaron's rod that budded, and the tables of the covenant.

Is it not interesting that God should choose to place the rod of Aaron inside such a holy place? Why not? Does not that which represents God's Holy Spirit deserve such position? The golden pot of manna typifies Jesus Christ as the bread of life and the tables of stone, or ten commandments typify the Father, the Lawgiver. Therefore, is it not fitting to complete the representation of the trinity with Aaron's "budded rod," typifying the precious Third Person of the Godhead—the Holy Spirit?

The Ark of the Covenant, which was placed behind the second veil, in the Holy of Holies, was a picture of our triune God dwelling among His people. Therefore, let us not exclude the Holy Spirit from the Holy of Holies; more importantly, let us not exclude Him from our lives and from our ministries.

chapter 6

The Chosen Vessel

But we have this treasure in earthen vessels,
that the excellency of the power may be of God,
and not of us.

II Corinthians 4:7

The Lord delights in using a life such as mine—one of weakness and filled with things that are despised and foolish in eyes of men. Although outwardly there appeared signs of weakness, inadequacy, and insecurity, deep down in the heart of this poor, naive, country boy, God was building a mighty faith and starting a fire that would burn inextinguishably within my breast.

God's plan for completeness begins with feebleness and uncertainty, and expands and develops to confidence and maturity. First he molds and shapes a perfect example, then replicates it. So the work that God was doing in my heart would be an example of what He could and would do in the life of every empty, broken vessel.

I am reminded of the scripture in Jeremiah 18:2-4, that records the sign given to Jeremiah:

> *Arise, and go down to the potter's house, and there I will cause thee to hear my words. Then I went down to the potter's house, and, behold, he wrought a work on the wheels. And the vessel that he made of clay was marred in the hand of the potter; so he made it again another vessel, as seemed good to the potter to make it.*

God must break the marred vessels; as we are crushed and can see ourselves as an irreparable vessel, He steps in and takes that soft clay and fashions and shapes us into the vessel of His choosing. He can make us a vessel of usefulness when we submit our will, ambition, strength, skill, talent, and knowledge to Him.

With me, unlike Moses, God did not have to spend forty years to undo what man had constructed. When God found me, He found a shattered vessel, with little potential of ever amounting to anything worthwhile. God delights to find a vessel that is broken and willing to place itself in The Hands of The Master.

When He needed a vessel to work through, He didn't go to the colleges and universities. He didn't go to the big city to find the rich or sophisticated, nor did he seek for the aged or mature. He came to a small farm in the hills of Pennsylvania, and there found a broken vessel hidden beneath the obscurity of an obtuse, poor, introverted, country boy.

I was born on August 12, 1949, the second of four children born of Robert and Irene Spencer. First came Sharon, then me, then Alan, two years later, and Brian, nine years later.

My parents provided an excellent childhood environment and upbringing on a small, 100-acre dairy farm. There was much love and happiness expressed in our home; however, one vital part was lacking, and that was a strong commitment to Jesus Christ. Through the faithful witness and concern of their pastor, my parents were encouraged to renew their commitment to Jesus Christ and bring their family into the church. I was nearly 12 years old before Christ became the center of our home, and through the church's Sunday School Department and the witness of my cousin, Dean, I accepted the Lord Jesus as my personal Saviour at the age of 13. I had felt the conviction of the Holy Spirit for some time, but did not understand that salvation comes by confession of my sins and simple faith in Jesus Christ. It was while sitting alone in a tree house that I had constructed in a large tree below the house, that I knelt down, and in simple, child-like faith, asked Jesus to become my Saviour. It would be several years before I would ever have the courage to openly confess what happened in my heart that day. Frankly, it was not until later that I fully understood what actually happened to me. Thus, through the influence of my parents and the church, I walked down the aisle to the altar and made a public confession of Jesus Christ as my Saviour.

Although physically I appeared to be a normal young boy, there was something unusual or backward about my personality. I had no desire to talk to or be around people. When strangers came to the farm, I would quickly withdraw and hide. When I became a little older, I would run out to the barn to be alone. Many people did not know that Bob and Irene Spencer had a boy named Randy, because I was so quiet and such a recluse. Most people didn't even know my name. I was simply referred to as "Bob's boy," the one you would see running to hide when visitors came to call. I was 10 years old before I ever spent a night away from home at my Grandma's house. I was only 5 miles from home, but it seemed like a thousand. And I'm sure it seemed at least that far to Dad when he had to come and get me at 2:00 a.m. Besides being homesick that night, I was also starved, because at supper time I chose to go hungry before I would ever say, "Pass the potatoes, please!"

There was no doubt that I felt very comfortable in the seclusion of the little farm in the country. However, when I had reached the age of seven, the inevitable had come. I remember my Mother's words: "I can't keep you out of school any longer. It is time you are enrolled in school." I'll never forget the first day of school and neither will many others involved with that experience.

The old '52 Chevy school bus came down the hill at Shucker's Orchard and stopped in front of our house. My heart began to pound and these thoughts raced through my mind: "They are going to take me away. I'll never see home again." My sister, Sharon, who had been in school 2 years by now, was standing on one side and my mother on the other. As the bus stopped, Sharon held my hand and pulled me on the bus while Mom held the other hand and pushed. After several minutes of struggle, and some assistance from the bus driver, I landed in the bus seat with my sister sitting on top of me.

Four miles down the road, the bus stopped in front of the one room schoolhouse. Picture, if you can, the schoolhouse as seen on the television program, *Little House on The Prairie*. This will give you an idea of the kind of setting in which I spent the next 6 years of my life. The old school had a bell on the roof which the teacher rang to summon the children to class. Inside was the old potbelly stove in the middle of the room, and the old water crock, with a hand dipper, that everyone gathered around during recess. Each desk was equipped with an ink well, fountain pen, and enough "Dick, Jane, and Sally" books to read for an eternity.

Outside the rear door was a well-worn path that led to the outhouse; beyond that was an open field where the softball diamond was located. Well, all this was certainly not impressive to a young lad being dragged off the bus and into the school each day. All I could think was, "When will I graduate and get this over with?" On opening day, the first-grade teacher was amused at my behavior when my sister led me to my seat and then started to her desk on the other side of the room, only to find me following close behind. For the next 4 weeks, I would sit next to her and never let her out of my sight. I became the boy that was seen, but not heard. When the teacher asked me a question, my sister had to respond with the answer. This became a pattern for me throughout the next 6 years.

While making my way through school as a little boy, I anxiously awaited the arrival of each weekend. I couldn't wait for the ole bell to ring on Friday. One of the things I anticipated most on the weekends, was riding my pony or my bicycle to Lonnie's house which was just 2 miles down the road. Then from his house we would ride together to his grandfather's farm. Lonnie, who was my cousin, was also such a close and dear friend. This meant that his grandfather, Otis, was my great uncle, whom I greatly admired.

Uncle Otis was among the first students to graduate from the Moody Bible Institute in Chicago, Ilinois. He labored faithfully in the field of evangelism and church

planting for over 60 years. He and his wife Electa were
filled with a fervor and fire for the Lord that was unexcelled.

Lonnie and I would play on their farm all day long. I
can still remember my Aunt Electa's evening call from the
front porch to come and eat supper with them. Lonnie and
I would sit at the table, and Uncle Otis would have everyone
hold hands as he would ask God's blessing upon the evening
meal. Uncle Otis was truly a man of God, and Aunt Electa
was one of the most saintly ladies I've ever known. They
had labored for years in the Lord's work, traveling through
the South, holding tent revivals and preaching in the streets.
Aunt Electa would play an old portable organ while Uncle
Otis played his guitar and sang. Soon, the crowds would
gather to listen, and Uncle Otis would take his Bible and
preach "hell-fire and brimstone" sermons, one after another.
I've been told that Uncle Otis would preach up and down
the streets of town until his clothes would be soaked with
perspiration and his voice completely gone. It has been said
that as he preached, he would saturate as many as a dozen
handkerchiefs, wringing them out and hanging them over
parking meters to dry. As he preached with power and
authority, many lives were touched through his ministry.
It was in the Bible Fellowship Church which he built in
1953 that I would later be saved and discipled.

As Lonnie and I sat at the table with this dear couple,
we realized their days of fiery preaching were nearly over.
Uncle Otis would say to Lonnie as he picked up his Bible,
"You know boys, I'm getting old and I can't preach much
longer. Someone will have to take up this Word and preach
it!" After supper, I remember that we would all go into
the parlor where the piano was located and Aunt Electa
would play the old hymns, while we sang. Uncle Otis would
get his guitar and say, "Now you boys need to learn to

play the guitar—it will help in your ministry." I sat there thinking to myself, "He doesn't know what he is saying. Me preach the Bible? I can't even say my name out loud without blushing!" I didn't say much, but I did listen intently to Uncle Otis' remarks.

Lonnie and I finally learned to play the guitar at Uncle Otis' house. Many Saturdays we would stay up late playing and learning new chords. Frequently, Uncle Otis would stop and say, "Boys, let's pray and ask God to place a call on your lives to preach the Gospel." He would reach out and lay his worn hand upon my shoulder, or upon my head, and pray: "Oh Lord, touch these boys and call them to preach, fill them with your Spirit, cause them to take up the *staff!* Amen."

I didn't understand his words as he prayed and I certainly didn't understand why he was wasting his time talking to me about entering the ministry. I was just a poor, shy, country boy. What could I ever do? I must confess that many a night I went to bed with Uncle Otis' words ringing in my ears: "Give them thy *staff*, Oh, Lord!"

In the ensuing years, I found myself attending my parents' church. Our entire family was now saved and we were growing and maturing in spiritual things. In October, 1965, during a revival service, Dad stepped out of the pew, followed by his entire family, and went to the altar of that little country church and dedicated his family to the Lord. Shortly following that, during a weekend church camp retreat, I felt the call to preach the gospel. My pastor had asked me to preach the evening message at church. At the young age of 15, I preached my first sermon, using as my text Philippians 1:21:

For to me to live is Christ, and to die is gain.

Many people in my church had never heard me speak a word, let alone preach a sermon. I was so backward and shy that it seemed like an impossibility. But you know, that's exactly what God desired to do—the impossible!

God was passing the *staff* from one of His great servants to a timid, pitifully inadequate young boy. Oh, that men would realize that what was about to happen was a work of God, not of man!

I'm reminded of the account of the little boy who came to Jesus with his small lunch of five barley loaves and two fish. As the multitude of hungry people gathered, Jesus questioned the disciples about feeding them. Philip said:

> *Two hundred denarii's worth of bread is not sufficient for them, that everyone of them may take a little.*
>
> (John 6:7)

Andrew, finding a young lad in the crowd who had five loaves and two small fishes asked the question, *But, Lord what are they among so many?* The young lad then gave what he had to Jesus. As inadequate and insufficient as it seemed, Jesus multiplied it and fed 5,000 that day. *What are they, among so many?* They are all that Jesus needs, if only they are presented to Him in faith.

I felt very much like that young lad who gave his lunch to Jesus. I said, "Lord, I don't have much to give, and what little I have is so insufficient; but Lord, it is yours." Praise the Lord! I can truly say today that God has used my life to minister to thousands who are hungry and thirsty for the truth. Through God's power in my life and His miracle of multiplying the "little things," He has used me to touch many lives for Christ through the multifaceted ministry in the church where I now pastor. A ministry that includes tent revivals, a gospel quartet, summer youth camps, the printed word, and a vigorously growing radio ministry. He took that little life so frail, timid, and broken and multiplied it to feed the multitudes. Glory to His Name!

I attribute everything that has ever been accomplished in my life and ministry to the *staff* that was placed in my hand. In the flesh, I can do nothing! In God's Spirit, I can do all things.

1 Kings 19:19-20 states:

> *So he (Elijah) departed from there, and found Elisha, the son of Shaphat, who was plowing with twelve yoke of oxen before him, and he with the twelfth; and Elijah passed by him, and cast his mantle upon him. And he left the oxen, and ran after Elijah . . .*

Do you see how God loves to call farmers? As Elijah is taken to heaven in a whirlwind and his mantle is falling to the dirt, Elisha quickly takes up the mantle.

> *And he took the mantle of Elijah that fell from him, and smote the waters, and said, Where is the Lord God of Elijah? And when he also had smitten the waters, they parted to the one side and to the other; and Elisha went over* (2 Kings 2:14).

Elisha prayed for a double portion of Elijah's spirit and he received it! The *staff* of Elijah was now in the hands of Elisha.

Several years ago I preached a series of sermons on the lives of Elijah and Elisha and found it enlightening to compare the miracles that God performed through Elijah to those He performed through the life of Elisha. I estimated that God performed twice as many miracles through Elisha's ministry, and 1 and 2 Kings contains nearly twice the written pages to record the exploits of Elisha as compared to the life of Elijah. Elisha truly received a double portion! The beautiful truth is obvious: God is not only looking for available vessels willing to be filled, but He is looking for those that wish to be doubly full.

God will fill every available space in your life that you submit to Him. Our lives and our ministries are limited only because we fail to offer to God our all. God is only as big in your life as the space you give Him to possess. Someone once said that in order to be filled with the Spirit, we needed more of the Lord! I would disagree. You can have no more of God than what you now possess, but rather He needs more of you. God has already given His all to us; it is we who need to give our all to Him.

Could you expand the volume of your life by pouring sin and self out? God will not fill a dirty, polluted vessel. Would you be broken and spilled out for Him? God can fill in a moment what it takes years to empty out.

Elisha saw how God was able to use Elijah, the empty vessel, and Elisha in absolute surrender cried, "Lord, use me twice as much and fill me doubly full!" Only God can take an empty vessel and fill it to twice its volume. He can do it for you . . . if you'll ask!

CHOSEN VESSEL

The Master was searching for a vessel to use
Before Him were many
Which one would He choose?

"Take me," cried the gold one,
"I'm shiny and bright
I'm of great value and I do things just right.
My beauty and luster will outshine the rest,
And for someone like you, Master
Gold would be best."

The Master passed on with no words at all,
And looked at a silver urn narrow and tall,
"I'll serve you, dear Master, I'll pour out your wine
I'll be on your table whenever you dine.
My lines are so graceful,
My carvings so true,
And silver will always compliment you."

Unheeding, the Master passed on to the brass,
Wide-mouthed and shallow and polished like glass.
"Here! Here!" cried the vessel "I know I will do,
Place me on your table for all men to view."
"Look at me," cried the goblet of crystal so clear
"My transparency shows my contents so dear.
Though fragile, am I, I will serve you with pride
And I'm sure I'll be happy in your house to abide."

The Master came next to a vessel of wood
Polished and carved, it solidly stood.
"You may use me, dear Master."
The wooden bowl said,
"But I'd rather you used me for fruit, not for bread."

Then the Master looked down and saw a vessel of clay.
Empty and broken it helplessly lay.
No hope had this vessel
That the Master might choose.
To cleanse, and make whole, to fill and to use.

"Ah, this is the vessel I've been hoping to find.
I'll mend it and use it and make it all mine.
I need not the vessel with pride of itself
Nor one that is narrow to sit on the shelf,

Nor one that is big-mouthed, shallow and loud,
Nor one that displays his contents so proud.
Nor one that thinks he can do all things just right,
But this plain earthly vessel, filled with power and might."

Then gently he filled the vessel of clay,
Mended and cleansed it, and filled it that day;
Spoke to it kindly—"There's work you must do—
Just pour out to others, as I pour into You."

                                            R.V. Cornwall

As I reflect back on my personal life, I am astounded
at the awesomeness of God. I realize how impossible it
is for the finite minds of men to comprehend the infiniteness
of the mind of God:

> *For my thoughts are not your thoughts, neither are your*
> *ways my ways, saith the Lord. For as the heavens are*
> *higher than the earth, so are my ways higher than your*
> *ways, and my thoughts than your thoughts.*
>
>   (Isaiah 55:8-9)

Human rationale and reasoning would use as the criteria
for choosing a vessel, the strongest, most appealing, most
costly one. God chooses the ugly, feeble, frail vessel,
as R.V. Cornwall writes so beautifully in his poem.
1 Corinthians 1:26-31 expresses it eloquently:

For ye see your calling, brethren, how that not many wise men after the flesh, not many mighty, not many noble, are called; But God hath chosen the foolish things of the world to confound the wise; and God hath chosen the weak things of the world to confound the things which are mighty; And base things of the world, and those things which are despised, hath God chosen, yea, and things which are not, to bring to nothing things that are, That no flesh should glory in his presence. But of him are ye in Christ Jesus, who of God is made unto us wisdom, and righteousness, and sanctification, and redemption; That, according as it is written, He that glorieth, let him glory in the Lord.

There could be no better commentary written about my personal life than what God has written in the previously quoted verses. It very accurately describes the story of my life. How, from the heap of human rubble, God retrieved what man considered worthless and irreparable, and from it, made something beautiful. My life stands as a living testimony of what God can do with what the world considers "a worthless refuse heap." To God be the Glory!

As a small child I felt very insecure and full of fear. The more rejection I experienced from my peers, the lower my self-image became. My self-esteem had reached its lowest point while I was a student in elementary school. The more I failed, the greater the feelings of rejection became until finally I felt totally worthless. I felt as though everyone looked upon me as the lowest in the class. As an athlete I always managed to finish last; and as for friends, they were few and far between. I was so introverted, I seemingly lacked any personality. The only recognition I ever received came during my senior year of high school when I was voted the most unlikely to succeed. The only security I felt came from within my home and family.

My mind seemed to be in a daze as I struggled through every day of school. One of my teachers felt it would be beneficial for me to repeat a grade. This just confirmed what I already felt in my heart—I was a failure.

Nothing seemed to work and no one could help me. Finally, the administration, not knowing how to cope with such a student as me, quietly passed me from one grade to the next. I think they had given up on me and wanted me out of the way. By the time I had completed the sixth grade, I felt like an illiterate. My ability to calculate problems in math was limited to the use of my fingers. Eventually, I was informed by Mr. Johnson that I was being recommended for placement in the special education department of the Junior High School for the following year because I would be able to "function better there."

However, Mr. Johnson was unaware that God was about to perform a "brain" transplant and Randy Spencer was about to receive the mind of Christ. I now understand and appreciate the full meaning of Philippians 2:5:

> *Let this mind be in you which was also in Christ Jesus.*

It was while I was in seventh grade that I began to excel and was promoted from special education through four different achievement levels until I finally reached the academic level. The teachers were amazed with my accomplishment. What made the difference? It was that year that I met Jesus Christ and I became a new creation and old things passed away and all things became new. I discovered a spiritual truth that would not only remain with me for the rest of my life but would have an impact upon my ensuing ministry. The more I saturated my mind and thoughts with the Word of God, the more my countenance and mind were transformed. One thing was certain: whatever was about to happen in my life, would have to be a work of God. There was no way that man could receive any credit for the resulting changes and success in my life.

As high school graduation drew near, I tried to ignore the call of God upon my life. Besides, I probably would never get into a Bible college anyway. No school was likely to accept me.

There were so many more qualified young people that God could choose. Why would He want me?

Countless times the Spirit of God tugged at my heart as I sat in the youth department of church. Each time I would ask, "Lord, why me?" I looked around at all the other boys who seemed more intelligent than I and were certainly more popular than I was. Some came from wealthy and influential families with great potential for success. Were they not better candidates for the ministry than I? No, God was not impressed with these qualifications. He had already chosen a poor, unattractive, frail, earthen vessel.

Besides, there was a war going on in Vietnam then, and chances were I would be drafted immediately following graduation in June 1968 along with every other able-bodied boy. The choice really wasn't to be mine. I knew that it would be made for me. I just knew that my last steps in the halls of high school would lead to the first steps in the halls of the U.S. Army—from the hayfields of my hometown to the rice paddies of Vietnam. Somehow, I knew my destiny was already determined. It really made it easy for me. I didn't have to think about what God wanted me to do with my life. I wouldn't have to make a choice after all.

It was at this time that the President of the United States, Richard Nixon, instituted a new system for the draft. It was known as the lottery system, and was to be conducted via television. According to the new system, all eligible young men eighteen years of age or older who had graduated from high school would be drafted in the order in which their birthdate was randomly drawn. The date for each day of the year was placed in the lottery barrel and, as each date was drawn, those whose birthdate matched were selected for the draft in that order. The first 100 birthdates drawn were to be drafted immediately. The next 100 drawn were very likely to be called within the next six months, and the third 100 drawn had a strong likelihood of not being drafted at all. Anyone with a birthday on the dates remaining after the first 300 would not be drafted.

I well remember that evening of the televised lottery. I was with several friends with whom I had just graduated. We had agreed to share the suspense together. We sat in silence, our ears pounding, with our eyes fixed on the television as the initial birthdates were drawn from the barrel. It's difficult to describe the feeling that we experienced that evening. Three of my close friends who graduated the year before me had already been killed in Vietnam, leaving many ugly, terrifying stories flooding my mind as I sat there waiting to see if my birthday, August 12th, would be selected.

Two of my friends who sat there that night were included among the first 100 drawn. As I continued to watch, I eventually found myself faced with different circumstances than I anticipated. My birthday was not selected until the 306th drawing. At this point, the probability of my being drafted was zero.

That evening I rejoiced in the fact that I had managed to escape the draft and the possibility of ending up in Vietnam. I was free to do as I wanted, or so I thought. However, I soon realized that it was only by the providence of God that my birthdate, August 12th, was not numbered among the first 300. He had a much greater plan for my life. Little did I know that I had already been drafted into another army—God's army, and that He had a very special plan for my life: He had a much higher calling for this boy born August 12, 1949. Basic training in the service of the King was about to begin for me. I knew that being a soldier in God's army would employ me for the rest of my life. There would be no discharge.

God has a very different and unique draft system. I might best describe it in the way it particularly applied to me: Upon entering the door of life, I noticed a sign written above the door, "Whosoever Will, May Enter." I freely made the choice and entered in through the door only to find that, once inside, an inscription above the door read "Randy Spencer, chosen before the foundation of the world." The scripture, found in Acts 2:21 bears this out:

> *That whosoever shall call on the name of the Lord shall be saved.*

Ephesians 1:4-5 further confirms our position in Him:

> *According as he hath chosen us in him before the foundation of the world, that we should be holy and without blame before him, in love Having predestinated us unto the adoption of sons by Jesus Christ to himself . . .*

Yes, I was drafted into God's service, yet I had to be freely willing to march in His army. Now I was faced with many important decisions that I must make. I had already received an application for enrollment in Appalachian Bible College. It seemed impossible that I would ever be accepted, and the whole idea of being a preacher was absurd!

At the time I had a part-time job working on a chicken farm about a mile up the road from home, working at something I enjoyed doing—plucking chickens and picking eggs. One evening as Dad was driving me to work, he said some things to me that will forever live in my memory. He reminded me of the importance of the decisions in life that I would now have to make and the effect they would have upon my destiny in life. He reminded me that although I had not anticipated the responsibility of having to make certain choices, now, as a result of God's intervention, the choices I was forced to make rested solely upon my shoulders. "Do you really believe that God so divinely directed the lottery to eliminate August 12th from among the first 300 birthdates chosen so that you could spend the rest of your life plucking chickens and picking eggs?" he had challenged.

Needless to say, that night at the chicken farm a battle raged within my spirit. God seemed to be reminding me that the time had come for me to make a choice. Was I willing to sell out to Him and serve Him, or was I going to go on my own way and do my own thing? What I did not realize at that time was that if I chose to serve the Lord He would empower me all the rest of the days of my life. I did not know that God was not looking for talent, ability, or great potential, but that all He wanted was a willing vessel. It has been said that God does not want our ability, He wants our availability.

In retrospect, I sometimes wish it were possible for me to look back and see what would have happened in my life had I not chosen to follow the Lord. Where would I be presently? I can only speculate, for only God knows what kind of life I would have lived without Him. However, I can testify as to what I do have today because I chose to serve the Lord. God has so richly blessed my life; it would take volumes to contain the list of blessings that He has showered upon me.

Once I made the choice to enroll in Bible college, God began to break and crush this vessel until there was no form or visage of the former self left within me. He began a remolding and rebuilding process to fashion me in the likeness and image that *He* had chosen. He changed a loser into a winner. He gave me a new heart, a new personality, a renewed mind, a new countenance, and a new life. This did not come without a lot of molding and shaping by the Master's hand. He alone provided me with everything I needed in preparation for my ministry. He gave me spiritual wisdom and discernment as He began to develop character and build a strong and mighty spirit within me. Although I did not fully realize what God was doing at that time, He was training me to lean upon the most important thing I needed for His work—the *staff*. Unless a man leans totally upon the power of the Spirit of God, he will never be fit for service.

*Take nothing for your journey, except a **staff** only.*
(Mark 6:8)

In 1968, I launched out with *staff* in hand and it's been a long journey ever since. I've been in the ministry for over 20 years now, and each year I realize more and more just how dependent I have become upon the *staff*. It would seem in the natural order of things that the older and more experienced one becomes, the more independent he becomes. On the contrary, that's not true with the servant of God. The older I become the more I realize, with each passing year, how much I need His *staff*.

Oh, how many times, during the earlier years of my ministry, I attempted to cast off the *staff* and rush ahead of God in the power of the flesh, only to fall and fail each time.

My first church was just such a training ground, where I learned not to rush ahead of God. He chose to place me in a very desolate, isolated area—a place where I could not, I suppose, do much damage. I sometimes think of it as my wilderness experience. It was to the pastorate of a little white, wooden-framed church in a West Virginia village with a population of 349. I wasn't ready for this church and, likewise, they were not ready for me. That little back hills country church will probably never forget the day this "greenhorn preacher boy" came to town.

I arrived in town with good intentions but perhaps a bit overzealous. I cast aside the *staff* which had sustained me up until this point and set out on my own to carry out "my" ministry. I thought I no longer needed this "crutch." I no sooner arrived than I began "preachin' " and carrying out my pastoral duties, beginning with home visitation. Within a matter of days, I had visited every home in town. I quickly informed the deacons of my plans to tear down the little, wooden-framed church and build a new one. I had envisioned plans for going on radio and television and initiating a bus ministry. Anyone with a dissenting attitude was expected to change, or leastwise, not interfere.

I foresaw great things happening at this church. I even pictured myself as another Jerry Falwell. Now in order to accomplish this vision, I knew I needed to work quickly and make many necessary changes. I remember the first change I attempted to make. It was the second or third Sunday after my arrival that I keenly watched what appeared to be a regular part of the weekly service. It made me uncomfortable, and I felt a change was in order. It was customary during the Sunday School hour to have those who had celebrated their birthday earlier that week to come to the front of the church and place one penny for each year of their age in a birthday bank, a bear shaped glass bottle, which probably had served at one time as a container for honey. Of course, the celebration of the birthdays was not complete without the singing of Happy Birthday while the procession marched down the aisle to place their money in the bank. After two Sundays, I concluded this to be a complete waste of time—God's and mine.

To prove my point, I roughly calculated the age of each of the presently enrolled members, and assessed the total age of the 35 members at 1,225. Now taking the total age of the congregation and mutiplying it by 1 cent, it was easy to figure the total collection for a year would yield $12.25. In my appraisal, this was certainly no way to raise money—the "birthday bear" had to go!

Drastic changes were in order, or so I thought. Without warning, I went to the church the following week and emptied all $4.20 worth in pennies into the offering plate and disposed of the little "honey bear" bank. Needless to say, when I entered the church on the following Sunday tension filled the air.

Noticing the absence of the bank, someone immediately asked of its whereabouts. At once, one of the deacons conjectured that the church secretary had probably taken it home to count the money, while some of the others began offering various other suggestions. I knew it was time for me to act as peacemaker and bring things under control.

Following the morning prayer, I tried as discreetly, yet as boldly as I knew how, to be the bearer of good news concerning the disappearance of the little bank. I tactfully explained that I had removed the bear, because I considered it to be a waste of God's time, as well as mine, and that valuable time was being wasted weekly with the foolish practice.

The immediate response from the congregation was negative to say the least. They were disgruntled and irate to think that I had such nerve to take such action, but I stood firm on my convictions.

Somehow, I managed to survive this experience. But I seemed to have an obsession for what I thought were necessary changes. However, with each change, I was just driving another nail into the lid of my coffin. Indeed, I will never forget the night I drove that final nail which led to my dismissal from the pastorate there. It came following a monthly congregational meeting on a Sunday evening. The deacon who was leading the meeting had waded through endless trivial items of business, from who was to ring the church bell each Sunday to how many were in favor of spending $5.95 for a new snow shovel. When he had finished, I assumed control of the meeting and informed the congregation that from that point on official business of the church would be conducted by a board made up of a group of men and the pastor—ladies excluded. With this I had sealed my fate.

My "empire" came crashing down after a brief period of only seven months. Late one night, this West Virginia village experienced a slight decrease in population. My wife, our baby daughter, and I made a quick midnight hour escape. We loaded a small U-haul trailer, hitched it to the back of our loaded car, and began our trek back to the only place we knew to go—home to Mom and Dad.

We soon learned how the Apostle Paul must have felt when he escaped by way of a basket from the city of Damascus. At least he had someone to hold the ropes, but we were alone, humanly speaking.

Feeling rejected, forsaken, and hurt, I needed time for my wounds to heal, so I dropped out of the ministry for several months. I was slowly beginning to understand that the ministry to which God had called me was not one of determination on my part but of dependence on Him. Without His *staff* to lean on, any and all efforts on my part would be in vain.

In time God called me to another church. It was a little country church located within a few miles of my hometown. It was there that God began to restore my vision and gently placed His *staff* back in my hand. I suppose, too, that I took comfort in the fact of knowing that, if things didn't work out in this church, I wasn't far from home.

This town was to become our home for the next 8 years. Much wiser now, following my "episode" at my former church, I was ready to submit to God and allow Him to work through me and use me as His instrument. God wanted to perform the work. It was His ministry, not mine.

God used the love, understanding, and patience of so many spiritually mature folks at this church to nurture me and help me to regain confidence and strength needed to continue my ministry.

Since we lived near my childhood home, I was able to minister to many of my family members and old high school friends. The greatest lesson that God wanted to instill in me was that the responsibility for results lay in His hands, not mine. In spite of all my past failures, God used me to build a great church in this town. What was once a small country church was eventually transformed into a strong, thriving work. I watched as God performed miracle after miracle, as land was purchased, buildings erected, and—ultimately—many souls saved. Many lives were transformed as a result of faithfulness in ministering the Word of God. As the congregation grew to nearly 500 people, God continually reminded me: "I will do the work, you will be the tool or available vessel."

There were so many wonderful and exciting things that took place. Yet there is one particular situation which overshadows all others. With the completion of our new church auditorium, we had used all the land we owned. If the church was to continue to grow, we needed to obtain land next to the church for parking space. There were only two apparent options: one was the vacant lot next to the church, and the other was a swamp land which obviously would be very costly to develop. The only feasible choice was the vacant lot.

Heedless of my past lessons and like I had done so many times before, I cast the *staff* aside and proceeded under my own strength. I went to the landowner of the vacant lot, explained to him the need of the church, and offered to pay what he thought was a fair price for the property. Without hesitation, he was quick to inform me that his land was not for sale and that he had no future intentions of selling any land to the church. I left with a broken spirit. What else could be done?

As the weeks passed, and parking conditions worsened, people were parking along the road and walking great distances to the church. Out of desperation I returned to make one last appeal, knowing all the while there was little money in the treasury. Yet I offered to pay whatever price the landowner would demand for the vacant lot. The response was the same—the land was not for sale.

Every effort seemed hopeless. I had exhausted all possible means. With no room for expansion, my ministry was at a standstill. Frustration and perplexity brought many sleepless nights as I lay awake trying to find a solution to the dilemma. Then, once again, that familiar, still small voice spoke to me, reminding me that I had been attempting to work things out in my own strength and had failed to depend upon His *staff*. To be honest, I had never even prayed about this matter. Without hesitation, I had proceeded in the flesh and, once again, had failed. As He had done so many times before, God patiently picked up the *staff* that I had so quickly thrown down, and once more placed it in my hand. I determined within myself that very night that I would cease in my attempts to solve this problem through human efforts and would pray and call God's people to prayer.

I met with the board and we prayed together. Then I called a special congregational prayer service, and one night after dark we walked to the property, encircled it with joined hands, and prayed. Until now, I had never fasted much, but I was so burdened about this need that I fasted three days and three nights. My every waking thought was consumed with the burden of this need.

I soon learned that when things are done God's way He will sometimes do the miraculous. The landowner of the adjacent swamp-infested property stopped by the church one day to tell me that for years he felt this land should be used by the church and offered to donate as much land as was needed for expansion. Although I knew it would take anywhere from 4-8 feet of solid landfill to make the land useful, I was confident this was directed of the Lord. We marked off several acres, and within days, the land became church property. To further show God's plan unfolding, I received a very unexpected telephone call from a man who owned and operated a coal stripping business. Somehow, he had heard of the church's need for fill dirt and offered to donate not only the fill but the trucks for hauling it and the equipment necessary for the construction of the parking lot. Furthermore, he wanted to begin immediately.

If there was ever a time I found myself speechless, it was then. I was so excited; I don't remember my exact response. Through the excitement he must have gotten my affirmative answer, because the very next day the project was underway.

What a sight! For days heavy equipment moved in and out of the site, until finally the project was complete and the parking lot ready for use.

But that's only part of the miracle. Soon the land which we had previously tried to purchase was placed on the market for sale and bids were being accepted. This was our opportunity.

Knowing that many people in the community knew of our interest in the land, I was sure someone would purchase the land and try to resell it to the church for a profit. Yet, God seemed to impress upon my heart that if we would make a reasonable bid, He would do the rest. Taking comfort in this fact, a bid in the amount of $1,000 was submitted by the church. Within days, a telephone call from a legal firm informed us that our bid was the only one submitted, and that the land was ours for $1,000.

Even to this day, the church has not used all the land that God provided during this time of total dependence upon Him. Oh how much easier, and wiser, it is for us to simply lean on His *staff* and let Him meet our needs.

Everything was going so well. The church had just completed a lovely new parsonage, and my wife and I were so happy there. Surrounded by family and friends, it was our home, but I knew that our happiness would only last as long as we followed God's direction. God does not let us rest on our past accomplishments. He continually wants to do more and more in our lives. Consequently, it was not easy to leave this church in 1982. Yet there was no doubt in my mind that God was calling me to serve elsewhere. His direction was now leading me to resign a very successful ministry and simply wait upon Him for further orders. Several months later, we left and moved about 50 miles away to pastor a little country church. We moved from a new home into an old rundown house— from a large, new church to a small church that was struggling financially and numerically. Words cannot describe how difficult it was to leave what we had worked so hard for and prayed so diligently to obtain. How could we begin all over again? But now, as I look back over the past 8 years of my present pastorate, I clearly see how God so beautifully worked out His will for us. There is no doubt that God had a greater work for us to do. As we were faithful to lean upon His *staff*, He has, and will continue, to use our ministry to reach thousands of lives.

I believe it was necessary for God to bring about these moves from place to place, so that I might learn my security was not in a church, or people, but in Him.

The *staff* is God's instrument for our journey, not for our lodging. I am only able to grow in faith and place confidence in His *staff* as I journey, and so God has always kept me moving ahead. Oh, how I have learned through the years that God will never lead me in any direction in which His *staff* will not sustain me. Christian, "take nothing for your journey, except a *staff* only."

Lean on His *staff*. Allow God to teach you to trust Him. Let Him lead you in the direction He wants you to go. You, too, can be His chosen vessel.

chapter 7

When The Staff Doesn't Work

Hopefully, this unusual approach toward the empowering ministry of the Holy Spirit will not be viewed by all who read it as sensationalism or over-spiritualizing the truth. The major focus is upon the recognition of the need for Spirit-anointing power. All the symbolisms are meaningless unless applied and practiced in the lives of Christians. How can this concept of *"The Staff of the Spirit"* be implemented in our daily walk with the Lord? Are these truths relevant and realistic? Can these spiritual precepts be contained by earthly vessels? I am confident that deeper understanding of these very simple truths will revolutionize your lifestyle, your relationship with the Lord, and your ministry or area of service.

Obviously, many struggle today with the issue of how one becomes spirit-filled and seek solutions on how to appropriate the power of God in their personal circumstances.

For certain, there are no secret formulas or magical incantations which can be devised to insure instantaneous success. It is with this thought in mind that I endeavor to establish useful guidelines and Biblical concepts that, when adhered to, will insure a life of victory. I believe these principles can, and should, be applied in the life of every Christian.

The *Staff of the Spirit* is not intended exclusively for the pastor, missionary, or full-time Christian worker, but for every believer, including students, teachers, choir members, deacons, homemakers, professional workers, and everyday laborers; *all* need the anointing of God for effectiveness in laboring in His fields. The need for each Spirit-filled believer is **POWER**. Power is needed to perform each and every task that God appoints. For the teacher, power manifests itself in the form of wisdom; for the singer, it's an anointed melody that stirs the listener; for the housewife, it is the radiant love to make her house truly a home; for the student, it's a fresh revelation of truth; and for the laborer, it is the quickening of the Spirit which brings a sense of God's presence to the workplace. This power is not only for public service and ministry, but for private and personal worship as well. It is the only means by which we may draw closer to Him.

Hence, one of the most important functions of the Spirit is to implant power for service within each believer. This power is made abundantly available to those who seek to be filled with God's Spirit. Paul the Apostle verifies this in 2 Corinthians 4:7 when he says:

But we have this treasure in earthen vessels, that the excellency of the power may be of God, and not of us.

Although the ministry of the Holy Spirit encompasses a multitude of activities, this book is dedicated to what I believe to be the most important facet of His ministry— the imparting of **power** for service. This hypothesis is substantiated by Paul in Ephesians 3:20 where he writes:

Now unto him who is able to do exceedingly abundantly above all that we ask or think, according to the power that worketh in us . . .

I believe it is clearly seen that the emphasis is upon the power of God which accomplished this.

The word *power* in the original Greek is *dunamis* which is the derivative of the word dynamite. Within each believer, this potential, explosive power is just waiting to be unleashed.

Why are so many Christians seemingly oblivious to this truth? Do they fail to recognize it, or are they indifferent toward it?

During my years of service in the ministry, I have witnessed multitudes of Christians who have reached their frustration point. The Word of God has little visible effect in their lives. Every futile attempt to establish a fruitful, effective ministry ends in defeat. The *staff* they hold in their hands is rendered powerless! Still others build ministries, direct many to Christ, disciple and motivate large numbers to service, and even perform miracles. Why are some successful, yet so many fail?

I have observed men of God who, after expounding and exhorting the Word, enjoyed the harvest of an outpouring of God's power. Their ability to handle God's Word with such authority caused even the strongest of Satan's demons to flee their presence. The awareness of God's presence was so prevalent that the entire audience was held spellbound.

On the opposite side of the coin, I have witnessed services which lacked that same power. Using the same Word, a similar text, and with a display of dynamic delivery, the pastor's words seemed to fall on deaf ears—failing to stir few, if any. Similarly, gospel musicians have masterfully presented their music; their singing was unequalled, each instrument was tuned to perfection, and a harmony sounded forth as though it came from heaven itself; yet, there was no moving of God's Spirit.

Ironically, I have been in services where average people, with average talent, have ministered in music and shared personal testimony, which touched the deepest recesses of my heart—causing my eyes to well up with tears and my soul to be stirred.

Why such a contrast? Why are some ministers of the Gospel effective and powerful, while others are ineffective and powerless? Why are some explosive like a stick of dynamite, yet, others fizzle out like a wet firecracker? How can one preach with the fire of the Holy Spirit, while the other becomes a smoldering smoke screen?

I would like to present three aspects which I consider imperative to obtaining power for service. The first prerequisite for acquiring this power is a genuine, born-again experience. Don't be so presumptuous as to believe that all who would attempt to serve the Lord are born-again Christians. Many well-meaning, hardworking, sincere individuals have futilely endeavored in service but have never been truly born again. There has never been a time and place when they recognized their sinful, lost condition and called upon the name of Jesus for salvation. They are sincerely zealous, but because they do not know Him personally, they *have a form of godliness but deny the power of it* (2 Timothy 3:5). This may seem an elementary truth, but there exists today multitudes who have ignored the Biblical way to God and have sought Him through the traditions of men. Theirs is a salvation of works rather than one of faith. Consequently, they are not true members of the family of God.

John 15:5 reads, *for without me (Jesus) ye can do* **Nothing**. In John 15 there is an analogy drawn between the grapevine and the Christian. Our heavenly Father is the vinedresser, or husbandman; Jesus is the vine; and Christians are the branches of that vine. The branches, which are to bear fruit, are of no value to the husbandman unless they are part of that vine. Certainly, branches cannot bear fruit independent of the tree itself, which is the source of their supply and gives life. In order to produce, one must, of necessity, be in Christ. For like the grapevine, productivity is dependent upon the branch abiding in that vine. Are you truly attached to the vine (Jesus)?

> *Abide in me (Jesus) and I in you. As the branch cannot bear fruit of itself, except it abide in the vine, no more can ye, except ye abide in me* (John 15:4).

Second, for the *staff* to work, one must be sure of the position of calling. I am fully persuaded that every believer has a specific purpose of calling. God saved you to place you into the Body of Christ as a specific member with a specific function. Romans 12:6 says:

> *Having then gifts differing according to the grace that is given to us . . .*

Paul the Apostle in Romans 12, stresses that every member of the Body of Christ is given a particular gift or function; some are given the ability to teach while others are given the gifts of faith, hospitality, giving, showing mercy, and helps, etc. There are many and varied spiritual gifts bestowed upon Christians, according to God's choosing. I will not proceed into an in-depth study on the subject of the spiritual gifts. Suffice it to say, you must discover through much prayer and communion with the Father, what your position, or calling, includes. 2 Peter 1:10 states:

> *Wherefore the rather, brethren, give diligence to make your calling and election sure; for if ye do these things, ye shall never fall.*

What a promise!

I sincerely believe that many failures exist because Christians attempt to operate outside the realm of their particular calling, or gift. God has chosen you to be a special part of His body; don't allow yourself to be dislocated through improper use. Don't try to perform in areas of ministry to which God has not called you or equipped you to serve. When we become willing to serve in the specific area of our calling, He will supply the necessary power to perform the task. Serving within the boundaries of God's calling will bring success and contentment. Trying to perform outside your specific calling will only lead to failure and frustration.

Christians, like athletes, must learn to play their position. Each participant is assigned to the postion that best fits his capabilities. Each member doing what he does best results in teamwork, and eventually, success for the entire team (body). A one-man basketball team, football team, etc., is destined to fail. It behooves us, as Christians, to learn to play our position (calling) and be satisfied that God has chosen us for that position. Not all Christians are singers, songwriters, preachers, teachers, or missionaries. Certainly, few have the ability to write and sing like Bill and Gloria Gaither; nor can we all preach like Billy Graham; or teach like Bill Gothard. We are assured that the Spirit equally distributes spiritual gifts, *to every man severally as he will* (1 Corinthians 12:11).

Let me share with you what can happen to one who tries to function outside this realm. I recall a young man, a God-called evangelist. He had tremendous ability to preach the gospel with a magnificent fervor and delivery. His countenance revealed the presence of the Holy Spirit. As an evangelist, he was abundantly gifted in charisma that attracted people to his ministry. He had an endless source of energy. In addition to all of this, he sang beautifully. His calling was confirmed by God's stamp of approval as multitudes came to Christ. I can testify, personally, to the special anointing evident in his ministry. This anointing had a marked affect on everyone with whom he came in contact, resulting in many lives touched and transformed.

Unfortunately, he became weary of travel and the pressure of evangelism. He thought the burden so great he chose willingly to depart from evangelism and decide to pursue, in the flesh, the pastorate of a local church. A short period of time spent as a local pastor ended in a sad commentary of failure and frustraton. Relying on his own abilities for the production of spiritual fruit, he experienced one failure after another. His ministry withered and he became a hindrance, rather than a benefactor to the work of God. All the gimmicks, self-induced activities, and attempts to generate results only led to defeat. As this once God-called evangelist, who had chosen to do his "own thing," continued in his fleshly attempts at pastoring, the waning of the Holy Spirit brought total devastation. He eventually left the ministry entirely—frustrated, defeated and forsaken. Today, as I write these words, my heart breaks for this man and my sincerest prayer is that one day he will be restored to his rightful position in the Body of Christ. This will only happen, however, when he lays aside all else, and becomes willing to once again serve within the guidelines of God's calling. The powerful *staff*, once held in his hand as an evangelist, was ineffective in his hand as a pastor. The *staff* is effective only in conjunction with the call.

I think it bears repeating. God's purpose is for every branch to abide in the vine and bear the intended fruit. An apple tree bears apples; a peach tree bears peaches; and a pear tree bears pears. Likewise, seek out your specific place of service and produce the fruit of God's choosing.

Third, for the *staff* to work effectively, there must be purity in heart and motive.

In 2 Kings 4:18-37, there is a most unusual order of events. The Shunammite woman, who had been so gracious and kind to Elisha in furnishing a room in which to stay, experienced tragedy in her own life. Her only son fell sick one day while working in the fields, and later that day died in the arms of his mother. The Shunammite woman, without hesitation, saddled a donkey and rode to find Elisha, the man of God. In verse 27, the woman falls at Elisha's feet and weeps bitterly, explaining to the man of God that her only son is dead. Then in verses 29-31 Elisha says to Gehazi, his servant:

> Gird up thy loins, and take my **staff** in thine hand, and go . . . and lay my **staff** upon the face of the child . . . but there was neither voice, nor hearing. Wherefore he (Gehazi) went again to meet him (Elisha), and told him, saying, The child has not awakened.

In other words, "here's your *staff* Elisha, take it back. It didn't work!" As the story continues, Elisha went alone into the child's room and shut the door and prayed unto the Lord. Elisha stretched himself upon the child and life was restored to the boy that very day. The joyous conclusion is in verse 37:

> *Then she* (the mother) *went in, and fell at his* (Elisha's) *feet, and bowed herself to the ground, and took up her son, and went out.*

The *staff* in the hand of Gehazi was worthless; it accomplished nothing. Why?

To understand the answer to the question in Gehazi's case, read 2 Kings, chapter 5. Gehazi had a severe problem in his heart that became evident as we briefly follow his life.

Naaman, the captain of the host of the king of Syria, came to Elisha to receive healing of his leprosy. He came proudly with money and clothing to pay for his healing. Remember how Elisha had instructed Naaman to go to the Jordan River and dip himself seven times, and his leprosy would be gone? God did touch Naaman, but it was by God's grace, not through Naaman's works. Naaman was sent on his way, having paid nothing. But Gehazi's greed got the best of him, so he ran after Naaman. When he finally caught Naaman, he lied to Naaman and said that Elisha had changed his mind and wanted the silver and changes of raiment. Obviously, Gehazi was not the man of God that Elisha was. So you can see Gehazi's problem was not with the *staff*, but in his heart.

We render ourselves useless in the service of God if there is sin in our lives. Why does the Word of God fail? Why do prayers go unanswered? Why are there no souls saved? Why are churches so dead? Why is there no power? We pick up the *staff*, shake it a few times and throw it aside and say, "Crazy stick, it just doesn't work!" However, the problem is not with the *staff!*

When ministries fail, out of sheer desperation we try other methods. We blame our people, or the area in which we are ministering. Perhaps a bus ministry, new hymnals, or an improved music program would cause great things to happen. The list goes on. In reality, equipment helps, but is incidental. It is useful to the pastor, but not vital. The best boat and outboard motor will not make a man a fisherman. The best airplane developed will not make a man a pilot. Neither will the best tools available make one a carpenter. Generators and modern electrical devices may brighten mission stations, but will not, of themselves, make light out of spiritual darkness. One may be attired in the finest of clothing and never bring the robe of righteousness to heathen hearts. The best radio equipment will not help a man hear from heaven. The finest medical training and equipment will not heal the brokenhearted. Without purity of heart, and *staff* in hand, we accomplish nothing. If the *staff* fails, before discarding it, examine your life, heart, and motives!

chapter 8

She's Got A Good Little Horn

I think every young boy longs for the arrival of his 16th birthday, so he can get his driver's license and purchase his own car. I think back to the '60s when I was a teenager. Having a driver's license held a little more appeal then, than it does today. Those were the days of hotrods, dragsters, and "souped-up" Chevelles. Remember these lyrics: "Little GTO, you're really looking fine, three deuces and a four speed, a custom 389?" Those were the days when every boy dreamed of having his very own "fast" piece of iron. Friday night in DuBois was cruising night; squealing tires with flashy hubcaps, and roaring engines with loud pipes. The cars that were really "in" were the '55 and '57 Chevys, and the '59 GTO's, the '55 Fords, and of course the Stingrays and Camaros. Well, when I turned 16, I didn't have any of those! I worked hard at Shucker's orchard picking apples for 75 cents an hour. I finally managed to save $60 dollars cash to buy my first car, a '57 Mercury. It wasn't exactly your "classic" sports car. It felt like it weighed more than a freight train and seemed like it was longer than a football field, although it was only 18 feet long. And, it had a two-speed, push-button automatic transmission, but at least it ran. Besides, once I put the final touches to it—baby-moon hubcaps, fox tails extending from the rear antennas, decorative spiders suspended from the mirror, and a raised front-end complementing a lowered rear-end suspension— I was ready to cruise. I'm sure those of you who were teenagers during the decade of the '60s remember all those fads.

At the same time I turned 16, my close friend, Jimmy, reached the same milestone. He didn't have quite as much money as I did, since he was fired from the job we had at Shucker's orchard for throwing apples at Mr. Shucker. He had managed, however, to save $35 dollars and was determined to buy a car.

One day, while riding the bus home from school, Jimmy spotted his "dream" car sitting in the back row at Chapman's Junkyard. It was special—a '53 Buick Special, in fact. Since the motor didn't run, it had to be towed home. He went that evening and bought it, towing it home with his Dad's old Hudson Hornet. The motor not working presented no problem for Jimmy; he knew he had the ability to fix it. He figured in a few short weeks he'd have it running like new.

I remember well the day that old Buick was towed home. Jimmy found a convenient location where he could easily work on it: under the old apple tree in the front yard. With the use of a block and tackle, he raised it up until he could stand under the car and work on the motor. However, getting his car on the road wasn't Jimmy's number one priority. He found "customizing" it a much more exciting job. First, he found a set of nice hubcaps; next, he had the glass tinted; then, he exchanged the automatic transmission for a 4-speed with a floor shift. Finally, using his allowance, he bought new floor mats, seat covers, and a new radio. During all this time, the car remained raised on blocks under the apple tree.

I used to go over to Jimmy's house on Friday night, and he would show me the new items he bought for the Buick. In order to get into the car, we used a six-foot stepladder, because Jimmy didn't want to remove it from the blocks until the motor had been repaired. All his friends climbed up into the car and admired all the fancy new things in it: the new mirror with fur around it, the fancy shifting knob, the seat covers and floor mats, the lighted gauges, and the suicide steering knob. We sat in the car with a light on, and the radio blasting out a familiar hit tune of the day, while Jimmy imagined himself driving through DuBois with all the girls staring and gaping. He pretended to be driving and shifting gears, while speeding through the quarter-mile, a thrill that challenged many young drivers in that day. Remember those days, gentlemen?

The next week, as I was driving by in my '57 Mercury, Jimmy stopped me. He wanted to show me another addition to his "dream" car. He had found an old "a-ooga" horn for the Buick. After listening to a few blasts from the horn, I asked the question, "Jimmy, when are you going to get the motor fixed and get this car on the road?" "Oh, I want to get it painted first; canary yellow with a glossy, midnight-black top," Jimmy said, with a gleam in his eye.

Well, that was 22 years ago, and to my knowledge, the Buick never did make it onto the road. Perhaps you can check sometime you happen to be passing through Luthersburg. Just look for a '53, canary-yellow Buick Special suspended from an apple tree. Jimmy may have never put it on the road, but "she's got a good little horn."

You know, I find this illustration humorous and rather amusing as I look back at some very wonderful days in my childhood. But, oh, how it typifies what I see happening in churches all across our country today. We spare no expense, or effort, in caring for the veneer, or appearance; but inside there is no power. All the paraphernalia looks nice, and sounds nice, but there is no power to move us.

Millions, and even billions, are spent on glass cathedrals, plush carpets, stained-glass windows, padded pews, and fleets of buses. The pastor is a dignified, professional man with more degrees than a thermometer. The candles are burning brightly, the choir is in perfect harmony, and the program working to perfection; but there is no anointing! We know when to stand, when to sit, when to kneel, and when to say, "Amen!" There are preludes, postludes, and interludes; but no dynamics. How impressive! But still no power!

I wonder how many churches in the world today are merrily blowing their horns? They look impressive and sound good, but there's no power, no anointing. I say that because it is possible to organize and operate the church and all its activities without the Holy Spirit. You can call a pastor, elect a board of deacons, buy or build a beautiful building, form a church choir, start a Sunday school and bus ministry, print your Sunday bulletin, and you're on your way! But are you? With the absence of the Holy Spirit it all leads to tragedy and unfruitfulness. 2 Timothy 3:5 says:

Having a form of godliness, but denying the power of it . . .

It is not by the eloquence of man, nor by education, or administrative skills, but it is by the Spirit of the Living God that mighty works are accomplished.

. . . Not by might, nor by power, but by my Spirit, saith the Lord . . . (Zechariah 4:6).

At Pentecost, Jesus told His disciples that they were to receive the Holy Spirit and *power*—the power to come after the Spirit had been given.

And ye shall receive power, after the Holy Spirit is come upon you; and ye shall be witnesses . . . (Acts 1:8).

We must remember we do not receive power, then the Holy Spirit. There can be no power void of the Holy Spirit. The Spirit comes upon powerless men to bestow His precious gift. This can be seen so vividly in the lives of the disciples. Before Pentecost, they were not able to walk in the calling Jesus committed to them. What a remarkable demonstration was effected in the before and after of Pentecost. Each of the disciples prior to Pentecost demonstrated greed, fear, anxiety, doubt, anger, carnality, pride, and a host of other sinful, unprofitable deeds of the flesh.

But after Pentecost, what a difference! In one sermon Peter witnessed 3,000 souls being converted. All the disciples now had boldness and power to stand firmly in their testimony. The power of evil forces was broken and the spiritual captives were released from bondage. The power of the flesh or sinful nature no longer controlled them. These men no longer submitted themselves to carnal deeds such as envy, strife, vainglory, pride, jealousy, all of which were evident before they received power from the Holy Spirit. The same Peter who denied his Lord and cursed Him now boldly demonstrated a zeal and boldness that ultimately led to his faithfulness unto death. I believe God purposely chose to use the disciples' lives to demonstrate the difference that not only the cross made, but what Pentecost did! Oh, they were saved and under the blood, but were not effective in their respective ministries till after the Holy Spirit came into their hearts and lives in His wondrous fullness.

Today, many churches are "sitting on the blocks" yet, in spite of it all, we extend an invitation to our friends to visit our services. They become spectators while we go through the motions. The preacher is at the controls, the organ is playing, the choir is singing, and the bright lights are flashing, but we are not moving. Sometimes, even the most sincere ministers, who want to see their churches active and alive, will attempt to stir their people to involvement with their encouraging words: "All right, everybody out and PUSH!" It's just about that time some skeptic passes by, hears the commotion, and remarks, "What's wrong with the motor?" We reply, "We haven't taken the time to fix that but, listen, she's got a good little horn!"

chapter 9

God's Broken Staff

And I will feed the flock of slaughter, even you, Oh poor of the flock. And I took unto me two staves; the one I called Beauty, and the other I called Bands; and I fed the flock (Zechariah 11:7).

And I took my staff, even Beauty, and cut it asunder, that I might break my covenant which I made with all the peoples.

And it was broken in that day; and so the poor of the flock that waited upon me knew that it was the word of the Lord.

And I said unto them, If ye think good, give me my price; and if not, forbear. So they weighed for my price thirty pieces of silver (Zechariah 11:10-12).

Then I cut asunder mine other staff, even Bands, that I might break the brotherhood between Judah and Israel.
Zechariah 11:14

In Zechariah 11 there is an interesting Old Testament parable which prophesies the rejection of God's Son, Jesus. The things which I find most impressive about this passage are found in verses 7, 10, and 14. Speaking in verse 7, the Lord says:

> *... And I took unto me two staves; the one I called Beauty (graciousness), and the other I called Bands (unifier); and I fed the flock ... And I took my* **staff,** *even Beauty, and cut it asunder, that I might break my covenant which I had made with all the peoples ... Then I cut asunder mine other* **staff,** *even Bands ...*

There seems to be no question in the former part of this passage that God is speaking about Jesus and his gift to humanity. In order that this gift of God might be given, He (Jesus) had to broken, or cut asunder. God allowed His *staff,* called Beauty, to be broken on the cruel cross of Calvary; to die for the sins of man. Isaiah 53:4-5 says:

> *Surely he hath borne our griefs, and carried our sorrows; yet we did esteem him stricken, smitten of God, and afflicted. But he was wounded for our transgressions, he was bruised for our iniquities, the chastisement for our peace was upon him, and with his stripes we are healed.*

> *Wail fir trees; for the cedar is fallen ... wail, Oh ye oaks of Bashan; for the forest of the vintage is come down.*
> (Zechariah 11:2)

Jesus, the very Son of God, left heaven's splendor and condescended to take upon Himself the form of a servant and die a common criminal's death on the cross. God gave His very best to die for our sins. God allowed His *staff,* Beauty, to be broken for us. Zechariah 11:12 even bears record of the price for which Jesus was to be sold:

> *I said unto them, If ye think good, give me my price; and if not, forbear. So they weighed for my price thirty pieces of silver.*

Jesus is referred to in many Old Testament scriptures as God's "Branch:"

And there shall come forth a rod out of the stem of Jesse, and a Branch shall grow out of his roots.
(Isaiah 11:1)

. . . Raise unto David a righteous Branch . . .
(Jeremiah 23:5)

. . . I will bring forth my servant, the Branch.
(Zechariah 3:8)

This truth is illustrated in 2 Kings 6:1-7, where the sons of the prophet were cutting trees near the Jordan River when an axe head loosened from the handle and fell into the water. The man of God, Elisha, was summoned to help. He instructed that a branch be cut, and cast into the water; and "the iron did swim." This illustrates how the human heart is as iron: when it is separated from God, like the axe head separated from its handle, it falls into the water of sin, lost forever unless God retrieves it. Jesus, "The Branch," was cut off from the riches and glories of heaven, and cast into this world of sin, so that now the stony, iron heart of man may be rescued from those drowning waters of sin. The hand of God through His Son reached down to reclaim lost humanity.

Jesus truly was "The Righteous Branch," a *staff* that was broken for us. These thoughts are so simply expressed in the words of the familiar hymn:

I was sinking deep in sin, far from the peaceful shore.
Very deeply stained within, sinking to rise no more.
But the Master of the sea, heard my despairing cry.
From the water lifted me, now safe am I.

James Rowe

According to Zechariah, God has two staves or *staffs*—
one is called Beauty, and the other is called Bands. It is
interesting to note in Exodus, chapter 27, that God instructed
Moses, when building the wilderness tabernacle, to build
the furniture in such a manner that it could be carried by
two staves, or *staffs*. The Brazen Altars, the Table of
Shewbread, and the Ark of the Covenant were transported
by two staves. God's present work, just as in times past,
is carried by two staves. One is Jesus Christ, His own Son,
and the other is the Holy Spirit, the Third Person of the
Trinity. Yes, the Holy Spirit was sent to do a great work
indeed—to live in the hearts of men. God found it necessary
to break His other *staff*, His Spirit, the one called Bands.
He (the Holy Spirit) left the glories of heaven and came
to earth to live in the confines of sinful hearts. What a
drastic change of residency from heaven to humanity; from
the bosom of the Father, to the body of every believer.
God cut asunder the Spirit and sent Him to earth to bind
believers together in unity and oneness, to bring to one
accord the broken Body of Christ, and to gather the
fragmented body parts to unite them under one Head, Jesus.
Is it any wonder God called him Bands?

When God sent His first *staff*, Jesus; He was rejected,
despised, and oppressed by men. Finally, he was placed
on a rugged cross where nails were driven through His
hands and feet, His side was pierced, and He was left alone
to die. Man crucified God's precious gift. His *staff*, called
Beauty, was broken again! Today friends, I ask you, "What
will you do with His other *staff*, His Spirit?"

We are warned in Matthew 12:31-32:

> *Wherefore, I say unto you, All manner of sin and
> blasphemy shall be forgiven men; but the blasphemy against
> the Holy Spirit shall not be forgiven men. And whosoever*

speaketh a word against the Son of man, it shall be forgiven him; but whosoever speaketh against the Holy Spirit, it shall not be forgiven him, neither in this age, neither in the age to come.

Since the dawn of creation, the Triune God has fervently endeavored to reach out to, and rescue, fallen man. The redemptive work of God the Father can be traced from Genesis through Revelation.

Beginning with the fall of man in the Garden of Eden, it was God, himself, who came to earth to provide forgiveness. When Adam sinned through disobedience to God's command, the Father, *made coats of skins and clothed them* (Genesis 3:21). It was the Father's plan, through the shedding of the blood of innocent animals, to provide a sin covering. Yet, Adam and Eve's son, Cain, like many today, rejected this plan of redemption.

In the New Testament, the Father sent *His only begotten Son* to redeem mankind. The Lord Jesus was rejected and crucified; yet, still men refuse His offer of forgiveness.

Finally, following the Ascension, God sent forth His Holy Spirit to draw men to Christ. His ministry is one of *conviction of sins, righteousness and judgment* (John 16:8). But there are those who continue to reject, grieve, and quench the Third Person of the Godhead.

In summary, God has always provided for atonement: in the Old Testament, through the shedding of the blood of innocent animals; in the New Testament, through His only begotten Son, drawn by the convicting power of the Holy Spirit.

Despite man's efforts to find the way to God, whether through tradition or other means, God's plan is forever settled and secure. Yet, men continue to break (quench) the *Staff of the Spirit.*

It is without difficulty that we are able to understand the brokenness of Jesus because He, like us, had a physical body of human flesh. Jesus, in His humanity, possessed a personality, an intellect, emotions, and a will. Rejected, He was broken and despised of men.

How then, is it possible for the Holy Spirit, who hath not a physical body, to be broken? The answer lies in the fact that He, too, is a person possessing the same traits as did Jesus—intellect, emotions, and a will. He, too, is saddened, repulsed, and grieved when rejected of men (Ephesians 4:30).

A vital part of the spirit-filled life is the privilege of fellowshipping with the Spirit. Fellowship demands emotional involvement. Joy, excitement, laughter, tears, sorrow, and every other emotion, under the control of the Spirit of God, are experiences to be employed and enjoyed by every child of God.

You have heard it stated many times that we are not saved by feelings but by faith. "God's Word says I'm saved. I believe it, and that settles it!" is a frequently quoted phrase familiar to us all. Although this certainly is true, I would like to further elaborate on this subject with the following illustration.

In the marriage covenant with my wife, Lynn, our feelings and attitudes toward one another, are equally important, if not more so, than the legal aspect of our union. However, if the success of our marriage was dependent upon nothing more than a marriage certificate, it would be a miserable relationship, indeed. Needless to say, there is a much sweeter side to our marriage. The emotional part of our relationship—the joy of sharing together in the good times, and comforting one another in the less fortunate times is the bond which makes our marriage meaningful and fulfilling.

Today, there are many slumbering churches and lackadaisical Christians who need a "Spirit-FILLED" relationship with God as well as a "Spirit-FEELED" relationship.

Many Christians view the Holy Spirit as some impersonal force, influence, or power, and fail to recognize His position as the Third Person within the Trinity. To quench or grieve the Spirit, is to break God's *staff.*

I can attest, through personal testimony, that when I sought the infilling of the Holy Spirit, my life and ministry were drastically changed. He (the Spirit) gave me a rejuvenated love for the ministry and instilled within me a compassion for others that I had not previously experienced. As I learned to respond warmly and sensitively to His guidance, my relationship with Him was then founded upon love rather than simple, Biblical fact. This verse became meaningful for me, personally:

And the disciples were filled with joy, and with the Holy Spirit (Acts 13:52),

In 1 Thessalonians 1:5-6, the total ministry of the Holy Spirit is revealed:

*For our gospel came not unto you in **word only**, but also **in power**, and in the **Holy Spirit**, and in much assurance . . . having received the word in **much affliction**, **with joy** of the Holy Spirit.*

When I experienced the infilling of the Holy Spirit, I realized that the fullness meant that the Gospel did not come to me in Word only, but exactly as described by Paul— in power, in assurance, in much affliction, and in joy of the Holy Spirit. My friend, that is the Spirit-filled life!

In conclusion, I redirect your thinking to yet another unique concept of the *Staff of the Spirit.* The physical *staff* provided a constant, abiding Companion with its continual, daily use; similarly, it is important for the believer to recognize the Holy Spirit as a necessary Companion for everyday living. The uniqueness of the *staff* lies in the fact that it symbolizes the continual and progressive daily walk of each believer.

Being filled with the Spirit is not a one-time experience, final and all-inclusive. There is a distinction between the salvation experience and the experience of being filled with the Spirit. The Christian life begins with the salvation experience, which is instantaneous, once, and final. Indwelt by the Holy Spirit at salvation, the infilling of the Holy Spirit occurs as growth and maturity develop within the life of the believer. The Spirit-filled life is one of continued yielding to God; not one neatly packaged experience. The assistance of the *staff* is necessary for the successful completion of this pilgrim journey.

A.W. Tozer, in his book, *That Incredible Christian*, expresses these thoughts very closely. The following various excerpts are from the chapter, entitled: "The Inadequacy of 'Instant Christianity.' "

"It is hardly a matter of wonder that the country that gave the world instant tea and instant coffee should be the one to give it instant Christianity. If these two beverages were not actually invented in the United States, it was certainly here that they received the advertising impetus that has made them known to most of the civilized world. And it cannot be denied that it was American Fundamentalism that brought instant Christianity to the gospel churches . . . .

"By 'Instant Christianity' I mean the kind found almost everywhere in gospel circles and which is born of the notion that we may discharge our total obligation to our own souls by one act of faith, or at most by two, and be relieved thereafter of all anxiety about our spiritual condition. We are saints by calling, our teachers keep telling us, and we are permitted to infer from this that there is no reason to seek to be saints by character. An automatic, once-for-all quality is present here that is completely out of mode with the faith of the New Testament . . . .

"In this error, as in most others, there lies a certain amount of truth imperfectly understood. It is true that conversion to Christ may be and often is sudden . . . .

"But the trouble is that we tend to put our trust in our experiences and as a consequence misread the entire New Testament. We are constantly being exhorted to make the decision, to settle the matter now, to get the whole thing taken care of at once— and those who exhort us are right in doing so. There are decisions that can be and should be made once and for all. There are personal matters that can be settled instantaneously by a determined act of the will in response to Bible-grounded faith. No one would want to deny this; certainly not I.

"The questions before us is, 'Just how much can be accomplished in that one act of faith? How much yet remains to be done and how far can a single decision take us?'

"Instant Christianity tends to make the faith act terminal and so smothers the desire for spiritual advances. It fails to understand the true nature of Christian life, which is not static but dynamic and expanding. It overlooks the fact that a new Christian is a living organism as certainly as a new baby is, and must have nourishment and exercise to assure normal growth . . . .

"By trying to pack all of salvation into one experience, or two, the advocates of instant Christianity flaunt the law of development which runs through all nature. They ignore the sanctifying effects of suffering, cross-carrying, and practical obedience. They pass by the need for spiritual training, the necessity of forming right religious habits and the need to wrestle against the world, the devil, and the flesh.

"Undue preoccupation with the initial act of believing has created in some a psychology of contentment, or at least of non-expectation. To many it has imparted a mood of disappointment with the Christian faith. God seems too far away, the world too near, and the flesh too powerful to resist.

"Others are glad to accept the assurance of automatic blessedness. It relieves them of the need to watch and fight and pray, and sets them free to enjoy this world while waiting for the next.

"Instant Christianity is twentieth century orthodoxy . . . ." [1]

The book of Acts describes how Paul and his co-laborers in Christ were filled with the Holy Spirit. It was a progressive sanctification, a continuous, never-ending process. Simply put, the Christian must be filled with the Spirit again and again.

The lives of the disciples clearly support this truth. In Acts 2:4, they were all filled with the Spirit in a prayer meeting held in an upper room (Acts 4:31). Then again, these same individuals were filled with the Spirit in Acts 13:52.

The *staff* is the ever-present Spirit, filling and empowering the believer throughout every stage of spiritual growth toward the ultimate—spiritual maturity. This same *staff* was instrumental in my own salvation by rescuing me from the clutches of spiritual death. It then became a Walking Stick which aided and directed me as a new believer to walk uprightly.

As I have continued on my journey of the Spirit-filled life, the *staff* has become my rod of correction and discipline enabling me to grow in the grace and knowledge of Him. As I've matured in the faith, I've learned to rest entirely upon the *staff* as my all-sufficient source.

It (the *staff*) became my weapon against the onslaught of enemies common to all of God's children—the world, the flesh, and the devil. The stronger I grew in the Lord, the more heated the spiritual battle became. Finally, I allowed the *staff* to become my sceptre of spiritual authority in Christ. As the Word says: *thou hast been faithful over a few things, I will make thee ruler over many things* (Matthew 25:21).

No finer example illustrates this so explicitly than John Bunyan's classic book, *Pilgrim's Progress*. Using the fictional characters Christian, Faithful, Hopeful, Christiana and others, his allegorical book depicts the pilgrim's journey through life. It focuses on the varied experiences of Christian as he journeys from the City of Destruction to Mount Zion. Bunyan also depicts the exceedingly narrow pathways and the pitfalls of Doubting Castle, Giant Despair, By-path Meadows and many others. After reading this compelling allegory, one should see the parallel betweeen the continuous spiritual growth of the character, Christian, and the born-again Christian of today.

At the risk of sounding critical, although I assure you that is not my intention, there was one thing, I feel, that was missing in Christian's journey to the Celestial City—the use of a *staff*. Having read this book, would you not agree?

Truly, the Spirit of God has given each pilgrim a "walking stick" to be used as a guide to the Celestial City. If we allow Him, He will help us on this pilgrimage through life. The *staff* will deliver us from the "City of Destruction" and protect us from sliding down the slopes of "Hill Difficulty." He will shield us from the wicked monster, "Apollyon," and preserve us from the "Slough of Despond." Yes, the *staff* of the Spirit will direct us along the treacherous slopes and through the narrow passageways. He will cause our feet to walk on "Delectable Mountains" where we may behold the beautiful gardens and orchards and drink freely from the fresh fountains of Living Waters.

Oh, dear reader, secure the *staff* tightly! Wrap your hand around the *staff* and grip it firmly so that when the battle is over and we have reached that "Celestial City," it might be said of you: He fought till his hand clave unto the sword *(staff)*. See 2 Samuel 23:10.

Many wonder what it is going to be like in heaven. There are those who envision St. Peter standing at the pearly gates questioning all who seek entrance. Others view a Great White Throne upon which God sits with a scale and balance weighing all their good and bad deeds. Still others view getting to heaven as a successful struggle to cross a cold, muddy river, to reach the other side where it is warm and dry. It's also been viewed as a journey through a long dark tunnel to emerge in a place where it is pleasant, sunny and bright. Or perhaps you vision a spirit with angel wings strumming a golden harp as he sits amidst a fluffy white cloud. But my view of heaven is having angels carry my body from this ole world in the very presence of the Father. As they set me before His throne, they'll say, "Here's your servant—one of Christ's redeemed. There's only one problem—he's got this ole stick in his hand. We couldn't take it from him." Of which I'll humbly reply, "Father, it's that *staff* you gave me years ago. I wanted to return it to you personally. With both hands I've held it tight. It was my comfort in troubled times. It was my guide down new paths. It was my rescue in distressing situations. It was my cool water in hot dry land. It was my *staff of Life* when I was hungry. It was my only defense against the enemy; and, as I walked through life, I rested heavily upon the top of this old *staff*. Thank you, Father, for sending me this comforter. I could not have completed my course without it. I now want you to have it back, Lord. It has brought me safely through. I won't be needing it any longer, for my journey is ended and I am safely home." With a tear in my eye, I'd like to say, "Lord, here's Your *staff!* I'm sure there's another weary pilgrim who can use it on his journey home."

[1] Taken from the book, *That Incredible Christian* by A. W. Tozer, Copyright ©1978, Christian Publications, Camp Hill, Pennsylvania, Used by permission.

Books & Tapes by Starburst Publishers

Except For A Staff   —Randy R. Spencer

Parallels the various functions of the Old Testament shepherd's staff with the ever-present ministry of the Holy Spirit. It sheds new light on the role of the Holy Spirit in the life of the Christian. "You will be blessed and challenged through reading *Except For A Staff,*" Rev. Jerry Falwell.

(trade paper) ISBN 0914984349   **$7.95**

Dragon Slaying For Parents   —Tom Prinz, M.S.

Subtitled: Removing The Excess Baggage So You Can Be The Parent You Want To Be. Shows how Dragons such as Codependency, Low Self-Esteem and other hidden factors interfere with effective parenting. This book by a marriage, family, and child counselor, is for all parents—to assist them with the difficult task of raising responsible and confident children in the 1990's. It is written especially for parents who believe they have "tried everything!"

(trade paper) ISBN 0914984357   **$9.95**

The Quest For Truth (novel)   —Ken Johnson

A book designed to lead the reader to a realization that there is no solution to the world's problems, nor is there a purpose to life, apart from Jesus Christ. It is the story of a young man on a symbolic journey in search of happiness and the meaning of life.

(trade paper) ISBN 0914984217   **$7.95**

The Beast Of The East   —Alvin M. Shifflett

Asks the questions: Has the Church become involved in a 'late date' comfort mode—expecting to be 'raptured' before the Scuds fall? Should we prepare for a long and arduous Desert Storm to Armageddon battle? Are we ignoring John 16:33, *"In this world you will have trouble?"* (NIV)

(trade paper) ISBN 0914984411   **$6.95**

TemperaMysticism—Exploding the Temperament Theory   —Shirley Ann Miller

Former Astrologer reveals how Christians (including some well-respected leaders) are being lured into the occult by practicing the Temperaments (Sanguine, Choleric, Phlegmatic, and Melancholy) and other New Age personality typologies. Texe Marrs says, "I highly recommend this book for anyone who truly desires to quicken one's discernment of the true things of God."

(trade paper) ISBN 0914984306   **$8.95**

Allergy Cooking With Ease   —Nicolette N. Dumke

A book designed to provide a wide variety of recipes to meet many different types of dietary and social needs, and, whenever possible, save you time in food preparation. Includes: recipes for those special foods that most food allergy patients think they will never eat again, timesaving tricks, and Allergen Avoidance Index.

(trade paper-lay flat) ISBN 091498442X   **$12.95**

Reverse The Curse In Your Life   —Joan Hake Robie

A handy "guidebook" for those who wish to avoid Satan's snares. Includes Biblical Curses, Forbidden Practices, Warfare Prayers, and much more. This book is the result of author Joan Hake Robie's over ten years of research on the subject of the occult, demons, and Satanism.

(trade paper) ISBN 0914984241 **$7.95**

Like A Bulging Wall   —Robert Borrud

Will you survive the 1990's economic crash? This book shows how debt, greed, and covetousness, along with a lifestyle beyond our means, has brought about an explosive situation in this country. Gives "call" from God to prepare for judgement in America, Also Lists TOP-RATED U.S. BANKS and SAVINGS & LOANS. D. James Kennedy writes, "This book on the current economic crisis makes good sense and is a timely warning to Christians to prepare for what could be very hard times ahead."

(trade paper) ISBN 0914984284 **$8.95**

Teenage Mutant Ninja Turtles Exposed! —Joan Hake Robie

Looks closely at the national popularity of Teenage Mutant Ninja Turtles. Tells what they teach and how this "turtle" philosophy affects children (and adults) mentally, emotionally, socially, morally, and spiritually. The book gives the answer to what we can do about the problem.

(trade paper) ISBN 0914984314 **$5.95**

What To Do When The Bill Collector Calls!
Know Your Rights   —David L. Kelcher, Jr.

Reveals the unfair debt collection practices that some agencies use and how this has led to the invasion of privacy, bankruptcy, marital instability, and the loss of jobs. The reader is told what he can do about the problem.

(trade paper) ISBN 0914984322 **$9.95**

The Quick Job Hunt Guide   —Robert D. Siedle

Gives techniques to use when looking for a job. Networking, Following the Ten-Day Plan, and Avoiding the Personnel Department, are some of the ways to "land that job!"

(trade paper) ISBN 0914984330 **$7.95**

The Truth About Dungeons And Dragons
—Joan Hake Robie

Explains the game of Dungeons and Dragons and lists the bizarre cast of characters which includes demons, dragons, witches, zombies, harpies, gnomes and creatures who cast spells and exercise supernatural powers. It tells how Dungeons and Dragons dabbles in the occult, encourages sex and violence and is a form of Devil worship.

(trade paper) ISBN 0914984373 **$5.95**

The Truth About Dungeons And Dragons—audio
—Joan Hake Robie

60 minute audio cassette narrated by Joan Hake Robie, author of the book *The Truth About Dungeons And Dragons.*

(audio cassette tape) ISBN 091498425X **$7.95**

Courting The King Of Terrors
—Frank Carl
with Joan Hake Robie

Why are so many people turning to Mental, Spiritual and Physical suicide? This book probes the relentless ills that are destroying the American family, and offers counsel to families in crisis. "I know about suicide," says Frank Carl. "I lost a Brother and a Sister to that monster!"

(trade paper) ISBN 0914984187 **$7.95**

The Rock Report
—Fletcher A. Brothers

An "uncensored" look into today's Rock Music scene—provides the reader with the necessary information and illustrations to make intelligent decisions about rock music and its influence on the mind.

(trade paper) ISBN 0914984136 **$6.95**

Man And Wife For Life
—Joseph Kanzlemar, Ed.D.

A penetrating and often humorous look into real life situations of married people. Helps the reader get a new understanding of the problems and relationships within marriage.

(trade paper) ISBN 0914984233 **$7.95**

A Candle In Darkness (novel)
—June Livesay

A heartwarming novel (based on fact), set in the mountains of Ecuador. This book is filled with love, suspense, and intrigue. The first in a series of books by June Livesay.

(trade paper) ISBN 0914984225 **$8.95**

The Subtle Snare
—Joan Hake Robie

You read about the PTL Scandal . . . Now read about the solution. This book will cause you to examine your own life so that you may avoid *The Subtle Snare*

(trade paper) ISBN 0914984128 **$8.95**

Inch by Inch . . . Is It a Cinch?
—Phyllis Miller

Is it a cinch to lose weight? If your answer is "NO," you must read this book. Read about the intimate details of one woman's struggle for love and acceptance.

(trade paper) ISBN 0914984152 **$8.95**

You Can Live In Divine Health
—Joyce Boisseau

Medical and Spiritual considerations concerning the dilemma of sickness. "Does the Christian have an inherited right to divine health?"

(trade paper) ISBN 0914984020 **$6.95**

Books & Tapes by Starburst Publishers—cont'd.

To My Jewish Friends With Love   —Christine Hyle

"One of the finest Jewish evangelism tools I have ever seen," writes Dr. Charles R. Taylor of TODAY IN BIBLE PROPHECY. Just slip this book into the hands of your Jewish friends and say, "I LOVE YOU."

(booklet) ISBN 0006028098   **$1.00**

Purchasing Information

<u>Listed books are available from your favorite Bookstore,</u> either from current stock or special order. You may also order direct from STARBURST PUBLISHERS. When ordering enclose full payment plus $2.00* for shipping and handling ($2.50* if Canada or Overseas). Payment in US Funds only. Please allow two to three weeks minimum (longer overseas) for delivery. Make checks payable to and mail to STARBURST PUBLISHERS, P.O. Box 4123, LANCASTER, PA 17604. **Prices subject to change without notice.** Catalog available upon request.

* We reserve the right to ship your order the least expensive way. If you desire first class (domestic) or air shipment (overseas) please enclose shipping funds as follows: First Class within the USA enclose $4.00, Airmail Canada enclose $5.00, and Overseas enclose 30% (minimum $5.00) of total order. All remittance must be in US Funds.   11-91